"I'm going to watch every step you take."

Lora shrugged. "Maybe I'll keep an eye on *you* to make sure you're as noble as you say you are."

Eyes flashing, Jon Woods, her newest challenge, said, "I'm not noble, I just know when someone is not who they appear to be."

She shook her head and walked back toward the house, aware that she should be unnerved by his threat, but feeling a shimmery thrill instead.

He was going to keep an eye on her, hmm? That should be interesting.

Okay, so she'd sworn off men.

That didn't mean she couldn't drive one remarkably irritating specimen a little crazy—did it?

She added a swish to her walk.

Take that!

Dear Reader,

Are you headed to the beach this summer? Don't forget to take along your sunblock—and this month's four new heartwarming love stories from Silhouette Romance!

Make Myrna Mackenzie's *The Black Knight's Bride* (SR #1722) the first book in your tote bag. This is the third story in THE BRIDES OF RED ROSE, a miniseries in which classic legends are retold in the voices of today's heroes and heroines. For a single mom fleeing her ex-husband, Red Rose seems like the perfect town—no men! But then she meets a brooding ex-soldier with a heart of gold....

In *Because of Baby* (SR #1723), a pixie becomes so enamored with a single dad and his adorable tot that she just might be willing to sacrifice her days of fun and frivolity for a human life of purpose...and love! Visit a world of magic and enchantment in the latest SOULMATES by Donna Clayton.

Even with the help of family and friends, this widower with a twelve-year-old daughter finds it difficult to think about the future—until a woman from his past moves in down the street. Rest and relaxation wouldn't be complete without the laughter and love in *The Daddy's Promise* (SR #1724) by Shirley Jump.

And while away the last of your long summer day with *Make Me a Match* (SR #1725) by Alice Sharpe. A feisty florist, once burned by love, is supposed to be finding a match for her mother and grandmother...not falling for the town's temporary vet! Matchmaking has never been so much fun.

What could be better than greeting summer with beach reading? Enjoy!

Mavis C. Allen
Associate Senior Editor

Please address questions and book requests to:
Silhouette Reader Service
U.S.: 3010 Walden Ave., P.O. Box 1325, Buffalo, NY 14269
Canadian: P.O. Box 609, Fort Erie, Ont. L2A 5X3

Make Me a Match

ALICE SHARPE

SILHOUETTE Romance®

Published by Silhouette Books

America's Publisher of Contemporary Romance

This book is dedicated to my husband
and his great, big wonderful heart.

Special thanks to Bill Weigle of Fogbelt Growers, for sharing
his love and knowledge of lily growing, and to my daughter,
Jennifer Jones, who helps me even when she doesn't know it.

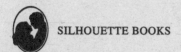 SILHOUETTE BOOKS

ISBN 0-373-19725-X

MAKE ME A MATCH

This edition published by arrangement with Harlequin Books S.A.

® and TM are trademarks of Harlequin Books S.A., used under license.
Trademarks indicated with ® are registered in the United States Patent
and Trademark Office, the Canadian Trade Marks Office and in other
countries.

Visit Silhouette Books at www.eHarlequin.com

Printed in U.S.A.

Books by Alice Sharpe

Silhouette Romance

Going to the Chapel #1137
Missing: One Bride #1212
Wife on His Doorstep #1304
Prim, Proper...Pregnant #1425
The Baby Season #1525
Make Me a Match #1725

Silhouette Yours Truly

If Wishes Were Heroes

ALICE SHARPE

met her husband-to-be on a cold, foggy beach in Northern California. One year later they were married. Their union has survived the rearing of two children, a handful of earthquakes registering over 6.5, numerous cats and a few special dogs, the latest of which is a yellow Lab named Annie Rose. Alice and her husband now live in a small rural town in Oregon, where she devotes the majority of her time to pursuing her second love, writing.

Alice loves to hear from readers. You can write her at P.O. Box 755, Brownsville, OR 97327. A SASE for reply is appreciated.

Lora Gifford's Matchmaking Agenda!

1. Grandma Ella: After the loss of Grandpa all those years ago, gossipy Granny _must_ be lonely. Besides, getting her a man of her own will take the focus off me! (I hope...)

2. Mom: With Dad out of the picture, Mom needs someone who can keep up with her full-of-life personality. Enter the dashing Dr. Reed. If only Mom would stop discussing the most unromantic things whenever she's with him. Is she _trying_ to ruin this for me   er, her?

3. Dr. Reed: Ten years older, and a whole lot more stable than Dad, the sweet and gentle vet would be the _perfect_ match for Mom. And a wonderful stepfather for me!

4. Dr. Jon Woods: Okay, so technically he already has a girlfriend, but wouldn't it be nice if she were actually in town? Well, not really, but at least that way I wouldn't find myself daydreaming about a future that could never be.

5. Me: This is the only way to get Mom and Grandma off my back! Pretend to be interested in a man—say, Jon Woods, for example— and hopefully they'll get the hint and leave my love life alone. Thankfully, Jon's agreed to the charade. Luckily my heart can't possibly get broken this time.**

    **[I'm such a liar.]

Chapter One

Clutching one very irritable tabby cat in her arms, Lora Gifford wondered who the heck the good-looking man walking through the examination room door might be.

The veterinarian she'd come to interrogate...er, meet? No way.

For one thing, this guy didn't appear to need the love of a good woman to whip him into shape. Besides, she had it on good authority that Dr. Reed was over sixty. This guy appeared to be half that age and what with his golden tan and chiseled features, looked more like a movie star than an animal doctor. Even the way he took off his wire rim glasses had star quality.

Drat.

Okay, back to plan B—whatever that might turn out to be. All she had to do now was figure out a graceful way of exiting, stage left. He smiled at her and another thought crossed her mind. What if this interloper had information? It might save time to just stay put and ask.

First things first, however. "*Who* are you?" she said, and because she hadn't intended her question to sound quite so much like an accusation, added, "It's just that I was expecting Doctor Victor Reed."

Mr. Hollywood folded his glasses into his breast pocket and extended a hand. "Victor's out of the office. I'm Jon Woods. I'll be happy to take a look at your cat this morning."

Intending to politely shake his hand, Lora relaxed her hold on Boggle, who took the opportunity to make for the hills. She gasped in pain as the cat's needle-like claws punctured the weave of her sweater, tearing holes in the tender flesh of her upper arm and shoulder.

Jon Woods gently unhooked Boggle and settled him on the stainless table with a practiced firmness the cat seemed to grudgingly respect. He rubbed Boggle's ears and crooned to him, his voice a soothing murmur. Was he speaking some kind of secret animal language? Tilting her head, Lora listened closely but couldn't make out a single word. Finally, keeping a good grip on his rebellious patient, Jon fixed Lora with a steady gaze. "Now, what seems to be wrong with Boggle?"

As far as Lora knew, there wasn't a thing wrong with Boggle that a horse tranquilizer wouldn't take care of. She wasn't there because of the cat; he was simply her cover. For that matter, he wasn't even her cat. She'd borrowed him from a neighbor. Rubbing what she imagined to be her blood-soaked shoulder, she glanced at the door and said, "I'll just wait until Dr. Reed gets back."

"You'll have a long wait. He had surgery on his foot so he'll be off for a few weeks."

"He's in the hospital?"

"Yes—"

"Good Samaritan?"

A quizzical look flashed across Jon's face, settling in his willow-bark brown eyes. "Are you another of his devoted admirers? No, wait, didn't I see on the chart that this is your first visit to the office?"

"I've never met Dr. Reed," she said. "I wouldn't know him from Adam."

He regarded her with open curiosity, which she tried to ignore. Striving for a casual tone, she added, "So, how long do you think the doctor will be in the hospital?"

"A few days, then he'll finish his recovery at home."

A new plan hatched itself in Lora's mind. She'd drop Boggle back at the neighbor's, then go into the shop and make up a flower arrangement and deliver it to the hospital herself. Better double check which hospital, just in case. As a florist, she did this all the time so that was no problem. Congratulating herself on the flexibility of her scheme, she cautiously started to pick up Boggle.

Jon's hand landed on hers. "I assure you I'm capable—"

"Oh, I didn't mean to insinuate that you couldn't fix Boggle."

He looked even more confused. "I'm sorry, they should have told you up front that you need to make an appointment for that procedure."

She liked the way his face reflected his emotions. She liked the way a lock of sun-bleached hair fell across his forehead. His hands, one of which still rested atop hers, were well formed, his touch extraordinarily light.

Lora worried her bottom lip. Was it possible this man was different from the rest? If he was a partner in this office didn't that suggest a certain stability? Maybe she should give him a chance....

No. No, no, no. "No," she said, aloud.

His hand slid off of hers and along Boggle's spine. Amazingly, the cat produced a tattered purr. Glancing at Lora, Jon said, "His temperament might improve if you did have him neutered, so you might want to consider it."

She'd forgotten that in the veterinary world, "fixed" and "neutered" were virtually synonymous. "I just mean that Boggle is—"

Boggle is what?

Since her sole experience with keeping pets revolved around the care of a twenty-gallon aquarium, she realized she'd neglected to think up a suitable ailment for the cat. Hoping to sound like less of a ditz than she suddenly felt, she mumbled, "Grouchy. I think he needs a checkup. He hisses...a lot."

"Is this new behavior for him?"

"Ah, no," she said, thinking of the times Boggle darted spiteful looks at her from beneath her neighbor's stairs. "No, he always seems ill-tempered."

"How about his appetite?"

How about his appetite? "Seems normal," she said.

"Any new members of the family to contend with?" he asked. "A husband, maybe? A new boyfriend?"

Was he flirting with her? She studied him but just couldn't tell. Should she invent a jealous spouse to squash any romantic notions that might be floating around in his handsome head? She murmured, "No husband."

"I see."

Their eyes met again. Lora looked down at the cat.

Jon opened a cupboard and brought out a pressurized can of cheddar cheese spread. He distributed a thin line of it on the table top which Boggle immediately began licking. Next the vet produced a stethoscope. "Okay, well, let's take a look at him," he said.

Lora couldn't help but admire the deft way Jon managed the examination. She wondered if Doctor Reed would have handled himself as competently. Surely he wouldn't look as good doing it. Jon was definitely in his prime, one could say. Strong. Competent. Great hands. She wished she'd paid more attention to how he looked in his glasses—she'd bet he was just cute as a button. If she could bend her neck a little, she could check out his rear—

Stop it! Concentrate on Dr. Reed.

For penitence, she began mentally building a flower arrangement in her mind. It was spring and the town of Fern Glen sat right on the coast, so Siberian Iris and dune grasses came to mind. Maybe daffodils. She'd never met a man who didn't like daffodils. At the hospital, she'd hide behind the arrangement just as she currently hid behind Boggle. She needed to find out four things: was Victor Reed likable? Did he have any obvious bad habits? Was he cute in an older guy kind of way? Was he available?

"Lora?"

Hearing her name snapped her out of her thoughts. "Huh?"

Jon looped the stethoscope casually around his neck. "I think Boggle is fine. Heart and lungs and stomach sound good, no other obvious problems. Of course, if you notice additional symptoms, bring him back in, but honestly, I think he's just ornery by nature. And he's already been neutered so I'm afraid that as far as personality goes, what you see is what you get."

He was probably wondering how in the world she would not know that her own cat was already neutered. She said, "Thanks, Doctor."

"Call me Jon."

She didn't want to call him Jon. She didn't want to call him anything.

Okay, that wasn't true. He was a tasty-looking dish, there was no denying that, but she'd recently bowed out of the dating game.

On the other hand, she didn't want to leave a bad impression even if she would never see him again. It was a small community and who knew when he'd show up at the flower shop needing flowers for some new honey? A beautiful bronzed blonde, she'd bet. A woman with long eyelashes *and* a thrilling career that didn't require she live from paycheck to paycheck. Sweeping aside wayward strands of wavy dark hair, Lora added, "Did I mention that I haven't had Boggle very long?"

"That explains a lot," he said as though relieved to discover she might not be a nitwit after all. He unfolded his glasses and put them on again, and sure enough, he looked fine. Reaching for the folder, he flipped it open and scanned the page. "It appears you forgot to give us your phone number," he said, glancing up.

"Why do you need my phone number?"

"It's office policy," he said, grabbing a pencil from the counter.

She mumbled out a bogus phone number and repeated her thanks. Clutching the angry cat and her checkbook, she hurried out of the small examination room only to be met by an assistant wearing a purple smock printed with frolicking dogs. The assistant told Lora to wait as she ducked into the room Lora had just vacated.

Lora more or less wedged an increasingly distressed Boggle between herself and a wall and wished she'd thought to bring a box. She tried stroking the cat's ears and crooning softly to calm him, just as she'd seen Jon do. For a moment, staring into eyes as green as her own, she thought she and the cat connected in some primal way, then he opened his mouth so wide she could see down his surprisingly pink gullet and emitted a hiss that made the hairs on the back of Lora's neck stand up.

"Bad kitty!" she scolded. With an annoyed glance at the examination room door, she wondered what was taking so long.

The assistant finally reappeared. "The doctor says there'll be no charge today."

Stunned by Jon Woods's generosity, she momentarily thought of tumbling to his charm, then she sucked it up and beat a hasty retreat. Once inside the van, Boggle crouched under the passenger seat and howled.

"No wonder I prefer tropical fish," Lora grumbled over the din.

* * *

Jon found himself looking out the window, angling for a glimpse of his last patient's owner.

All he saw was a big blue van pulling out of the parking lot. He resettled the blinds and picked up the folder beneath Lora's.

He'd been in Fern Glen, a quaint town on the Northern California coast, for a little over a month and face it, he'd been growing increasingly bored. There were just so many times a man could walk along a windswept beach—alone. Only so many times he could admire towering trees or chat with strangers. He missed Los Angeles, Trina, his own life, and not necessarily in that order.

He couldn't deny, however, that Lora Gifford had piqued his interest. She was just so…well, so *real*. He'd be willing to bet there wasn't a phony hair on her head, and speaking of hair, that ebony fall of glistening strands was unbelievable.

Lora. Her name was Lora and she seemed a little skittish, as though she'd been wounded in the past. He felt a protective surge in his chest and smiled at his own folly. His ability to empathize with creatures was a bonus in his career; he just had to guard the tendency to let it guide his reactions to people. Especially female people.

He put Lora Gifford out of his mind as he got ready for his next patient, a black Labrador puppy with the sniffles.

Five years before Lora was born her parents had purchased a small piece of real estate in the heart of Fern Glen. Her mother dreamed of opening a fabric store. Her father yearned to start a bait and tackle shop. They settled on a florist because at the time, Fern Glen didn't have one.

Compromise. That was the name of the game for her parents, but it hadn't come without taking a toll on their relationship. For all intents and purposes, Lora had grown up in a petal-lined war zone. In the off season, while her father fished and her mother made quilts for extra money,

Lora had escaped into after-school work with a local lily grower, her mentor a disabled old man with a wealth of experience he was anxious to share. For her, his warm glass-sided buildings had become a sanctuary.

Four years before, Lora had received a modest inheritance from a favorite uncle and shocked everyone by using it to buy herself a house. Her parents had been surprised by her choice—the house was small and ungainly. What Lora didn't explain was that she'd really bought the house because of the greenhouse out in back.

Two years later, her father decided thirty years of married life was enough, hooked up his boat and drove away. Her mother kept the shop. Lora, who discovered how limited the financial resources really were when she took over the books, invited her mother to move in with her for a few months. The months had turned into a year.

And then Lora's long-widowed grandmother had shown up on Lora's doorstep with three suitcases and five cardboard boxes, everything else she owned tucked safely in storage. She was lonely. How could Lora turn away her own grandmother? At least Grandma was willing to share a room with Lora's mom. So now three generations resided in Lora's little cottage and Lora was one breath away from going nuts.

It was Calvin's fault. The rat had left her, and in leaving her, he'd opened the door for her relatives to come charging through, a single goal firing their passion: find Lora a husband! It didn't matter how many times Lora told them she wasn't interested—they simply didn't believe her.

She'd been so sure that Calvin was "The One." They were the same age, he loved the outdoors as she did, he had family in Fern Glen. Perfect. Then he'd accepted a job in Chicago without even telling Lora he'd applied. All she had to do was pack a bag. He, it seemed, had a plan.

Only, she had plans of her own.

Take it or leave it, he'd said.

At that point she'd decided there was one thing of which she was certain: she was not going to follow her parents' example and spend her life compromising.

Now, thanks to the meddling of her loving relatives, a seemingly endless procession of quasi eligible men had recently shown up for dinner or come into the shop to buy flowers. Things were getting out of hand.

Out of desperation, Lora had given the matter some deep thought. Loneliness was the culprit, she decided, for both her mom and Gram, so she'd attack from that angle. With luck, she'd shift their attention away from her love life and on to their own.

After Lora dropped Boggle off, she entered the flower shop through the delivery door in the back. She tiptoed around, relieved to find her mother and grandmother busy with customers out front.

For a second, she thought about Jon Woods and his ploy to get her phone number, and she felt a smile threaten to emerge. She wiped the smile away with a firm wave of resolve. Sure he was interesting and as sexy as all get out. It wasn't that she was blind to his attributes, she reminded herself, she was just on the mend. It wasn't wise to flit from relationship to relationship like some dazed bumble bee.

But Jon is local, an animal doctor, a man with roots like your own, her subconscious needled. *Maybe you should let down your guard a little and get to know him....*

No. Concentrate on Mom and Gram. There'll be time to investigate Jon Woods in the months to come.

She checked the fax machine to see how behind they were. Not bad. After making a couple of calls to confirm which hospital Dr. Reed was at she quickly put together a suitable arrangement and made it out the door again without being detected.

At the nurses' station, she discovered Dr. Reed's surgery had been two days before, which was terrific news. Surely he'd be well on the way to recovery by now and perhaps a little lonely. Lonely people liked to chat, even to florists. She told the busy nurses she'd deliver the flowers herself. A few moments later, she got her first glimpse of her prospective stepfather.

Dr. Reed, lying in his bed, glanced up from a book the moment Lora came through the door. The first thing she noticed about him were the color of his eyes, a perfect match for grape hyacinths. A neatly trimmed beard and a full head of sterling silver hair accompanied the eyes—the man looked like the captain of a cruise ship!

"More flowers?" he said.

There were no other flowers in the room. "You bet. Where would you like them?"

"Who are they from?"

She'd thought of that. Picking out the card she read, "Says here they're from your friends at the Animal Clinic." She handed him the card and he studied it for a moment.

"Those guys really went overboard. I told my sister to take the other bouquets because I'm getting out this afternoon. Just put those by the window."

No aging girlfriend to schlep his flowers? Good.

"I'd be happy to deliver them to your house," she said, still holding the flowers and excited about the prospect of seeing how and where he lived.

"I couldn't ask—"

"I insist," she said. "So, you're going home. Are you thrilled?"

His eyes twinkled. "You bet."

"It'll be good to sit down in your own house with a fat cigar and a stiff drink, right?" *Was that too obvious a prying question?*

Apparently not. "Never have smoked though I do enjoy the occasional glass of red wine," he said, settling comfortably against his pillows. "They say it keeps you young."

"Looks as though it's working," she said with a grin.

He laughed. He had a nice laugh. "Now, what's a pretty girl like you doing flirting with an old goat like me?"

She laughed, too. She liked this guy. Hope began to flutter in her chest, and it wasn't just selfish hope anymore. Her mother deserved happiness, deserved to be with someone ten years older and wiser than she.

Lora said, "Do you live with your sister?"

"Oh, no," he said amiably. "Jess is married and has her own home. No, since my wife died and our two sons moved to the east coast, I live alone."

Lora gestured at his bandaged foot, which lay outside the covers. "How are you going to handle getting around by yourself?"

"Crutches."

"They can be difficult to get the hang of."

"Well, Jess will come by during the day and I'll be okay at night."

Genuinely concerned, she wrinkled her brow. "You'll be all alone? What if there's a fire? How will you manage by yourself? You should hire someone to stay with you. It's dangerous to be alone."

"Sounds as if you're in cahoots with my doctor and my sister, young lady."

"My name is Lora Gifford," she said, shifting the arrangement to her left arm and offering her right hand. She'd taken an immediate liking to this man and had big plans for his future that required him getting back on his feet ASAP. Her mother loved to dance.

He shook her hand. "Well, Lora, it's really no big deal. I don't mind being by myself."

No one to stay the night meant no girlfriend, right?

Let's see, she'd covered obvious bad habits, availability, appearance and charm. Was there anything else?

He looked from her to the card that had come with the flowers and back again. "Lora Gifford? Are you George Gifford's daughter?"

"You know my dad?"

"I used to fish with him years ago, back when my boys were just kids. He owned the Lora Dunes flower shop which I just realized he must have named after you."

"Me and the beach."

"I'll be. I remember seeing you with your mother a couple of times. You were four or five years old. Your mother was a beauty. Jet black hair, emerald eyes...you look just like her."

"She's still beautiful," Lora said fondly, wishing she did look like her mother, knowing she'd inherited her grandmother's demure stature and her father's nose. "She and dad are divorced now, but Mom's doing great."

"Well, I'll be," he mused, his eyes thoughtful. "Where is your dad?"

"Down in San Diego, fishing his heart out."

"I'm sorry about him and your mother."

Lora said, "It's okay. They're both happier now."

"And how about you? Married? Kids?"

"No, neither."

"I didn't think so, but so many young women keep their maiden name now and don't wear rings, you just never know."

While Dr. Reed seemed to study Lora, she chewed on her lip. Was it really possible this man was as decent as he seemed to be? Appearances could be so deceiving, and first impressions were worthless in the long haul. Besides, it wasn't as though she had a good track record with men, young or old or in-between. No way was she going to jeopardize her mother's out-of-practice heart on a guy whose pleasant manners hid the soul of a cad. She needed more information....

She said, "Dr. Reed, I have an idea. Sometimes I hire

out for odd jobs. You know, to make ends meet. I could come to your house after work. At least there'd be someone there at night in case a fire started or...something."

He looked quite startled by the abruptness of her offer. He wasn't the only startled one. What had she just done? She thought of her mother, she thought of Gram, truth be known, she thought of their next batch of erstwhile bachelors.

"I really am quite capable," she said firmly.

"I don't doubt it for a moment," he said.

"And I'm neat as a pin."

A smile curved his lips. Lora could sense him considering her suggestion.

"I go to bed early," Dr. Reed said. "It would be boring for you."

"Mom says only boring people get bored," she said, hoping to impress him with her mother's pithy insights. "I can provide references—"

"Not necessary," he said with a wave of his hand.

"What's not necessary?" a voice said from the doorway.

Lora recognized the voice and turned in time to find Jon Woods striding across the linoleum. He blinked rapidly when he saw her face.

He wasn't the only one blinking. Out of his office, with a tailored jacket thrown over his form-fitting black shirt and no stethoscope looped around his neck, he looked suave, sophisticated and harder than ever to resist.

Why had she bunched her hair into a ponytail before coming to the hospital? Why hadn't she taken off the lousy green sweater and replaced it with—anything else!

This yin and yang of her current position concerning men was disconcerting. Wanting and rejecting. Thinking *maybe* and then slamming the door.

Staring into her eyes, he said, "This is a coincidence, isn't it? I didn't expect to see you here."

His gaze made her damn near breathless but his arrival embarrassed the heck out of her. She'd not expected to see him again either, especially in the hospital room of a man she'd admitted she'd never met. She glanced at her watch and saw that it was the lunch hour—great planning on her part. This could get dicey. "I'm delivering flowers," she said.

"You two know each other?" Dr. Reed asked pleasantly.

Jon released Lora from his gaze. "We met today when she brought her cat in for a checkup. She was disappointed when I showed up instead of you, Victor."

Jon's remark was met with a wince from Lora and raised eyebrows from Dr. Reed who said, "I don't believe you've ever been to the clinic before, have you Lora? Don't tell me my memory is that bad."

Hadn't her mother told her to never lie? She'd used a lifetime's quota that day and now she was going to pay for it. Or maybe not. Looking at Dr. Reed, she said, "I heard all about you from my friend, Peg Ho. You're Cerise's vet." This was the truth and Lora felt suitably virtuous.

Dr. Reed chuckled. "Peg's Irish Setter is a dynamo."

Jon said, "If you enjoy animals with personalities, wait until you meet Lora's cat."

"Boggle tends to be a little antisocial," Lora said and added, "In fact, I'm thinking of letting my neighbor have him. She adores cats." Anxious to get the topic of conversation off of her pretend pet, she said, "I'm glad we ran into each other, Dr. Woods. I wanted to thank you for not charging me to examine Boggle."

"I asked you to call me Jon."

"Jon." Lora felt a sigh build in her throat and squelched it, but sometimes her new lifestyle choice was hard, and never more so than now. It didn't take even a good imagination—and hers was excellent—to picture herself wrapped in his powerful arms, held against his rock-hard chest, stroked with his gentle hands...

"Beautiful flowers," Jon said, admiring the arrangement.

"Lora's a florist," Dr. Reed said, his gaze traveling from Jon to Lora.

Jon smiled at her in such a way that her knees felt a little weak. She'd always been a sucker for a good smiler.

"Your work is original," he said.

"Thanks." She needed to get out of this room for more than one reason!

Jon looked over her head. "Victor, is there anything I can bring you this evening when I come back to visit? Magazines? A portable radio? Illicit milkshakes?"

"I'll be long gone by this evening," Dr. Reed said. "Jess and her husband are picking me up this afternoon."

"That's great news."

Lora saw her chance. "I'll leave you guys alone now," she said, and started to shuffle off. She and Dr. Reed hadn't firmed up anything concerning her wily plan to nurse him back on his feet and into her mother's heart; no doubt Jon's arrival had nixed the whole idea.

Jon gestured at her arms. "Aren't you going to leave the flowers?"

"Lora is bringing them to the house tonight," Dr. Reed said. "Not that these aren't appreciated, Jon, but really, you guys down at the clinic shouldn't have sent me any more flowers."

Jon's brow creased. "I don't think we did," he said.

"'Course you did," Dr. Reed said, handing Jon the card. "It says so right here."

Jon read the card.

"Maybe one of the assistants arranged it," Lora mumbled. She was going straight to hell for all these lies!

"Those girls are always going overboard," Dr. Reed said fondly.

Jon still looked skeptical.

"Fact is, this little lady is going to be my nighttime nurse for the next couple of weeks," Dr. Reed added with a wink at Lora, who grinned with pleasure.

Jon looked up from the card. "I thought you refused to have strangers in the house at night."

"Well, Lora isn't a stranger. I knew her father once upon a time."

"You knew her father?" His eyebrows inched up his forehead again as Lora tried to recall their earlier conversation at the clinic. No use; it was a blur. Jon said, "Victor, I would have been happy to help you out. You did so much for my dad."

"And now you're covering for me at the clinic. The debt is more than paid. Besides, you don't have time to play nursemaid and Lora is prettier than you are."

Both men stared at Lora who felt a red tide wash up her neck. "I can't argue that point," Jon said at last.

"And she'll let me pay her for her time, won't you, Lora?"

"Of course," she said breezily, thinking of a timing belt for the van.

"And now that I know Lora has a cat at home, I feel even better about my decision." Dr. Reed turned to Lora and added, "I'm glad you came in here and talked me into taking your help. You're very persuasive."

Lora smiled wanly as a sudden cold front engulfed Jon's inherent warmth. She could imagine what he was thinking. Why would she insist on staying with a man she'd never met before, one she'd quizzed him about just hours before? Finally, after an eternity or two, he said, "You talked him into it?"

"She all but insisted, didn't you, Lora?"

Jon's wary gaze make her feel like confessing her plot. *It's like this,* she could say. *Mom is lonely, I'll find someone for Gram later, I want my privacy back, Dr. Reed seems like a great guy and what better way to find out if he really is as nice as he seems than to hang around his house for a couple of weeks?*

Like that would make things better!

Jon's back was to Dr. Reed and he didn't bother to look cordial when she murmured goodbye. At the last minute he said, "I'm sure we'll meet again."

Not if she could help it!

Chapter Two

Lora stored the bouquet she'd take to Dr. Reed's later in the big walk-in refrigerator, taking a second to inhale deeply. As always, the cold, flowery air cleared her mind as it filled her lungs. So many flowers, so many choices, and the order she was filling simply gave a price range—the selection and composition was up to her.

As she arranged heavy copper roses with dark purple iris, lemon colored freesia and glossy magnolia leaves, she watched her mother and grandmother out of the corner of her eye and for the first time, had doubts about what she was doing.

They looked so…content.

Grandma Ella with her wispy white hair and rosy cheeks was dusting everything in sight, concentrating especially, it seemed to Lora, on items by the front door. No doubt Grandma had arranged some semiaccidental meeting between Lora and a friend's grandson and was looking for him even now. Groan.

Lora's mother, on the other hand, was busy helping a middle-aged man pick out the flowers for a bouquet to be wrapped in cellophane. At fifty, Angela Gifford was a tall, slender woman with glossy black hair barely brushed with gray, cut to ride atop her shoulders. She was by far the best of the three with customers, knowing when to help and when to back off. Grandma Ella tended to talk people to death and Lora had what her mother called "patience issues."

A few hours later they all drove home together, Lora at the wheel, the iris and daffodil arrangement secure in the rack in the far back, Grandma Ella chatting away about her friend's grandson.

Once inside the house, Lora broke her big news. "I have a job for two weeks," she informed them as she counted and fed her fish. All present and accounted for. Her denizens of the deep had survived another day.

"I'll be gone in the early evening until morning, I'm helping out an older guy who just had foot surgery. I'll still come into work, of course, and the money I make will fix up the van. One of you two is going to have to feed my fish."

Grandma Ella made tsking sounds deep in her throat. For years, Lora had tried to emulate these sounds as they seemed to come in quite useful in a variety of circumstances, but she just couldn't get them right. Grandma said it was because she didn't have enough bosom. Lora looked down at her chest. The fact that she wore an oversized sweater didn't help much, but maybe Grandma was right.

The tsking faded away and Grandma said, "I invited a young man over for dessert tonight, Lora. Oh, that's right, you were off making deliveries when he came in. You might want to comb your hair and change your clothes."

Lora's mom opened the refrigerator and took out a foil wrapped package of leftovers. No matter where she lived or with whom, Angela Gifford was a true cook, the kind who roasted a turkey and fixed all the trimmings for just two people, who got giddy if a friend presented her with a freshly caught crab.

"Chicken enchiladas okay with everyone for dinner?" Without waiting for an answer, she added, "I don't know, Mother, I thought the boy looked a little young."

This comment got Lora's attention. "How young?"

"Angela, when you get to be seventy-one, everyone looks young," Grandma Ella insisted.

"How much younger?" Lora asked warily.

Grandma shrugged plump shoulders. "I don't know."

"Six years if a day," Lora's mother said firmly.

Aghast, Lora blurted out, "Six years! I'm almost twenty-five years old! What's wrong, have you gone through every twenty-something male you know so now you want me to date teenagers?"

"I never noticed this age prejudice in you before," her grandmother tsked. "Besides, your mother is exaggerating."

Lora felt a scream coming on.

Lora's Mom shook her head. "Lora's right, he's too young."

Lora said, "Thank you, Mom." At last, reason.

"I want grandchildren," her mother continued. "What kind of money can a teenager earn unless he's a dot-com genius or in a rock band? Enough to support a family? I don't think so."

"Pauline assures me her godson has potential," Grandma Ella insisted.

Lora's mom clicked her tongue. "So does the new barber across the street and he's got his own business."

"Owning a barbershop is good," Grandma said. "No matter what happens, men will always need someone to cut their hair because there's not a one of them that can do a decent job of it himself unless he shaves his head. Okay, we'll just feed this boy some strawberry shortcake and shoo him on his way."

Angela nodded. "Good. By the way, Lora, I met the barber face-to-face this morning. His name is Michael. He's just delightful and listen to this—he asked about you!"

With renewed clarity, Lora knew that something had to give and it wasn't going to be her. She no longer cared that her mother and grandmother seemed happy in their matchmaking schemes—these women needed a different diversion than Lora's love life and what better diversion than a love life of their own!

She was back on track.

She said, "Grandma, I'm not going to be here for dinner or desert."

"But how will that look?"

Leaning over her grandmother and kissing her soft hair, she said, "Sweetie, it doesn't really matter how it looks." She assumed a stern expression and added, "I've repeatedly told you guys that for the time being, I've sworn off men. As for marriage and babies, just forget it. A woman isn't defined in the old ways anymore."

"But being part of a team is truly wonderful," Angela said with a sappy glow in her eyes. "A woman needs a man, honey. Sure, there are hard times, and I know Calvin hurt you when he ran off to Chicago. Trust me, I know about hurt. But that shouldn't sour you on all men."

Lora was speechless. Her mother's faith in the opposite sex, no matter how many times she'd been proven wrong, was astounding.

"Just stay and have dessert," Grandma Ella added as she hulled strawberries. "After this, I promise, no teenagers."

"I need to go out to the greenhouse," she said, gesturing at the cloudy glass structure in her backyard. "I'll lock up after myself out there and water in the mornings on my way to work. And don't forget to feed my fish." All this was said as Lora scribbled Dr. Reed's name and phone

number on a scrap of paper and shoved it into her mother's
hands. An hour later, greenhouse chores complete and
overnight bag packed, she pulled out of the driveway just
as a kid in a red convertible pulled in.

Victor Reed lived in a sprawling split-level house on the
outskirts of town. The huge yard was beautifully designed
with towering trees and lush foliage, including masses of
late-blooming rhododendrons, but everything was overgrown. Lora guessed that Dr. Reed's wife had been in
charge of the upkeep.

Her mother was a gardening wizard!

Two cats, one gray and white and the other coal-black,
sat on the front porch, smack in front of the door. A riot
of barking ensued at the sound of Lora's knock. She tried
the knob. Two large dogs charged outside as the two cats
darted inside. Lora juggled her suitcase and the flower arrangement as the dogs sniffed and wagged.

She had to yell. "Hello?"

"Back here," Dr. Reed called.

The big yellow dogs came back inside with Lora. A
third dog came charging down the hallway—this one
shaggy and about the size of a toaster oven. After a noncommittal growl, he licked her suitcase.

The same sense of good taste gone to seed permeated
the house. Apparently, Dr. Reed had let the whole shebang
get away from him. Well, she had a cure for that, didn't
she? Over the weekend, she'd get her mother to come over
to help weed and casually introduce her to Dr. Reed.
They'd stare into each other's eyes. Mom would see an
older man with laugh lines and a gentle heart and Dr. Reed
would see an attractive middle-aged woman with great legs
and a ready smile. The scenario played itself out in Lora's
head.

All that was left was to find grandma a match!

The dogs led Lora to a smallish room with dark leather

furniture and shelf upon shelf of books. A big desk sat in one corner, but Dr. Reed was sprawled on a recliner, his bandaged foot out in front, a blanket thrown over the rest of him. A different cat, this one pure white, slept on his lap. His crutches were on the floor beside his chair and a muted television flashed light into the room.

"You came just in time," Dr. Reed said. "I'm about to starve to death. Maybe you could order us a pizza."

"Or maybe I could just fix something," Lora said.

"Jess did the shopping. All she bought was real food."

"Real food?"

"As opposed to the stuff you can throw in the microwave. Can you cook?"

Stepping over the dogs that had settled on the rug, she put his flowers on the desk and dumped her suitcase out of the way. "Can I cook?" she scoffed. "Point the way to your kitchen."

Dr. Reed's sister had indeed stocked the refrigerator and within half an hour, Lora had stir-fried shrimp and asparagus and cooked a pot of jasmine rice. She made a tray for the both of them and took it back to the den. All the animals had settled close to Dr. Reed. In unison, they looked up as the aroma of food wafted across the room.

"Kick them out into the backyard," he said as she set the tray on a low table. "Just shake the treat jar by the back door, they'll come running. Don't worry, the yard is fenced. Boy, I'm sure glad you're used to animals."

Not those who actually had feet, she thought. Sure enough, the furry critters showed up with the first rattle of their treat jar. By the time she returned to the den, Dr. Reed was in the process of spearing a shrimp. "Who knew you could cook like this?" he said after tasting it. "You're so young."

"My mother taught me," Lora said. "She's a great cook. It's incredible she's kept her figure."

"She sounds like an amazing woman."

"Oh, she is," Lora gushed.

He smiled at her and they chatted while they ate. She discovered he'd been widowed for several years, that all his pets were former patients their owners had abandoned in one way or another and that he had a delightful attitude about life. In other words, he was the total opposite of her father. Lora beamed. Her mother was going to love this guy.

Lora felt so at home that when the doorbell rang she jumped up without waiting for Dr. Reed to ask her to get it. Through the glass panel, she could see Jon Woods standing on the porch, a duffel bag in his hand, an impatient look on his face.

What was he doing here?

She had half a mind to pretend no one was home, but that was stupid, he could see the Lora Dunes Florist van out front. That duffel bag was ominous, however, so steeling herself against his disdain, she opened the door.

"Where are the dogs?" he said.

What a greeting! It was obvious he was still suspicious of her. Lora smiled and said, "I poisoned them and buried them in the backyard. Want to see?"

He groaned and shook his head.

Had she really known him for just this one day, and how had he gone from being so nice to being so annoyed in such a short time?

Was it because she wasn't *trying* to make him like her? If so, it was obvious her own true personality wasn't exactly magic when it came to the opposite sex. The blasted sweater probably didn't help much, either. She vowed to get rid of it. Dating or not, a girl had her pride.

"What can I do for you?" she asked him.

"Not a thing," he said, and walked right past her into the house. His familiarity with the place was evident in the way he went directly to the den. Lora closed the door and followed him. He looked good from the back, his body strong and tall, his shoulders broad. He wore faded jeans and a black T-shirt and cross trainers on his feet. He had a way of walking that looked masculine and physically fit. That walk reminded her of Calvin. He walked the same way, with a subdued bounce, full of confidence, full of sass. Full of himself.

Dr. Reed greeted Jon with genuine warmth. "It's a shame you missed dinner," he said.

"I stopped off for a sandwich," John told him. "Where are the dogs?"

"In the backyard. Lora has a way with them. Well, it's too bad you ate. I think it only fair that as Lora got here first, she gets dibs on which bedroom she wants."

"You knew he was coming?" Lora asked.

"Of course. After you left today, Jon pointed out how much more useful he would be with some of the more personal aspects of my care, like bathing."

Though this was undoubtedly true, Lora glared at Jon.

"Happy to be of help," Jon said. His voice was nothing but sincere, but the challenging scowl he leveled at Lora said it all. "In fact, Victor," he added, "why don't we *let* Lora go home? I'm sure she has better things to do than hang around with a couple of veterinarians."

Lora came close to punching him.

"Absolutely not," Dr. Reed said just in time. "Lora and I made a deal. Besides, her mother taught her to cook. Imagine, asparagus and shrimp with ginger and garlic—well, she's a whiz. She even wants to weed the garden this Sunday. You'll be glad she's around during the long evenings when I'm out like a light by eight o''clock."

"I'm an excellent conversationalist," Lora said in an attempt to goad Jon. "And I play a mean game of strip poker."

Jon didn't crack.

Chuckling, Dr. Reed said, "See? Isn't she cute? Lora, I think it's time to let the dogs and cats back inside for the night. Jon, how about getting me a pain pill and helping me to bed?''

As Jon assisted Dr. Reed, Lora fumed and fussed her way back into the kitchen with a platter of dirty dishes and a bad temper. Jon was up to something, that much was clear. He didn't trust her, that's why he was really here.

Why should he trust you? a niggling voice chirped in the back of her mind.

"Oh, shut up!" she snarled.

The animals were all begging at the door. They came inside in one big whoosh, tails wagging, snouts nuzzling, bodies coiling around her legs.

It was startling being surrounded by so many critters! And, truth be known, a little comforting. Tropical fish didn't interact a lot and never when actually outside of their aquarium, of course, so this was all new. The white cat rubbed against Lora's shoe and Lora reached down and picked it up. The cat regarded her with a raspy purr and adoring blue eyes. Hard to believe she and Boggle belonged to the same species.

"The fact is," she whispered into the cat's ear, "I'm sneakier than Jon. I also have a lofty goal to fuel my fire— true love. Well, the possibility of true love, at least. Plus, I need to get those meddlesome females out of my life before they marry me off to the unsuspecting barber across the street. Or a teenager," she added with a shudder. "With all that going for me, why should I be worried about what Jon thinks or what Jon wants or even that he seems determined to interfere with my plans?"

The cat kneaded her claws and purred. If that wasn't a resounding vote of confidence, what was?

"The cat's deaf," Jon said from the doorway.

Startled, Lora twirled to face him. "What?"

"Frosty is deaf. White cats with blue eyes often are. The white gene can induce withering of the inner ear.

Frosty's former owners couldn't handle it, that's why Victor adopted him.''

"Oh. She's a him.''

"So spilling your guts to that cat is kind of pointless.''

Yikes! What had he heard her saying? Setting the cat down, she said, "How did you know I was spilling my guts, which I wasn't, by the way. Were you eavesdropping?''

He smiled. "Don't worry, I didn't hear a word. Listen, we have to talk. Come with me.''

She folded her arms across her chest. "We can talk right here.''

"No. Come outside.''

"It's dark out there.''

"Are you afraid of the dark?''

She wanted to say, *No, I'm afraid of you.* She said nothing.

"We'll turn on the porch light.''

Leaving the dogs at the door, they went into the backyard. Jon switched on a light and the overgrown path to a small structure at the far end of the yard glowed with soft light.

The structure turned out to be a garden gazebo, less than eight feet across with bench seats on three sides. It had probably been charming at one time, but the drizzly north coast weather had stripped it of most of the white paint and dry rot had tilted the foundation. Jon sat on one creaking bench and Lora sat on another.

While she waited for him to gather his thoughts, she admired the way the light hit his cheekbones and forehead and glinted off his hair. This was the north coast in April— no way his hair got sun-bleached around here unless he went to a tanning booth or had it artificially bleached and she just couldn't see him in either scenario. That meant he'd moved here from somewhere sunny and not too long ago.

Somewhere sunny. Him in a bathing suit, bare back crusted with glittering sand, sunlight warming his big shoulders. Suntan oil, warm ocean breezes, margaritas in a thermos. Her beside him—

What!

It was this setting. Romantic, hidden, the perfect place for crazy fantasies.

Another scene unfolded in her head. In this small drama, she was alone with Jon, not on the beach, not in the blazing sun, but here in this gazebo, the fragrance of flowers mingling with the nearby smell of the sea, his eyes smoldering as he looked deep into her soul. She could just about feel his fingers touch her face and the heat of his mouth as it closed over hers—

Jon cleared his throat and the wild images flitted away. Still, he said nothing.

"Not that this hasn't been fascinating," Lora said stiffly, now wanting to escape her imagination as much as a confrontation, "but if you'll excuse me, I'll be going to… well, bed." She rose to her feet.

"Drop the act," Jon said softly.

She sat back down. "What act?"

Now he stood. Pacing back and forth in small controlled steps, he shot her a laser-like glance. "I know what you're up to."

He did? "You do?"

"Yes. And I think it's appalling." The pacing stopped, the glance turned into a glare. "You're trying to con Victor into a marriage."

How did he know this? Lora racked her brain, trying to recall if she'd said anything to anyone about her plans for Dr. Reed and her mother. She hadn't, she was sure of it. Wait a second, she wasn't trying to con anyone, she was simply facilitating romance. There was a difference! Fired by righteous indignation, she said, "I don't know what you're talking about."

He laughed. "You're good, I'll give you that. When I first saw you this morning, I thought—well, it doesn't matter what I thought. You've been lying since the moment I met you. Boggle isn't even your cat, is he? That's why you didn't know much about him. You just used him to get close to Victor and when you found out he wasn't there, you grilled me about where he was. I tried calling you this afternoon—big surprise, the phone number you gave me turned out to be disconnected. You showed up at the hospital with flowers that no one at the clinic sent— I checked with all the employees so don't bother denying it. Now you've wormed your way into Victor's house."

As there was more than a grain of truth in what he said, Lora went on the offensive. "I'm not the one holding a secret meeting out in the backyard," she said. Not liking the disadvantage of her head being lower than his, she stood. She was still at a disadvantage as he was quite a bit taller than she but unless she climbed up on a bench, this was going to have to do.

"I'm not holding a secret meeting."

"Then why are we hiding out here?"

"So we won't disturb Victor."

"At least I treat him like an adult."

This remark earned her another glare. "Victor was my father's best friend. He was there for Dad when Dad got so sick he could barely work. Dad wouldn't tell me he was that sick, he didn't want to worry me. That's a laugh, isn't it? Well, at any rate, I owe Victor Reed big time. He's a decent, honest man. I won't stand by and watch you seduce him for his money."

Lora's eyes grew wide. Had she heard him right? "*Me* seduce him?" she gasped. "Is that what you think?"

"Of course. You're a gold digger. Admit it."

Lora was momentarily speechless. "That's…that's crazy," she finally sputtered. "He's old enough to be my—"

"Father," Jon said.

"Oh, this is ludicrous."

"Is it? How about the coquettish way you acted in his hospital room?"

"I don't even know how to act coquettish."

"You were managing just fine. Batting your eyelashes, giggling…he may look old to you, but he's a man, and a man, especially an older man, is susceptible to a pretty young woman coming on to him, taking him flowers, offering to care for him in his hour of need, cooking his favorite dinner. I don't even want to know how you figured out what he liked to eat. Who did you pump for that information, his sister, his sons? No, don't tell me. And, by the way, this meeting isn't a secret. Tomorrow morning, I'll tell Victor everything you say tonight, so I guess you'd better pack your bag and go home, the party is over."

While she admired his loyalty and spunk, he was definitely endangering her plans and more to the point, the conclusion he had reached about her motives was downright insulting. If she told him the real reason she was interested in Victor Reed, would it make a difference? Sure, he might think slightly better of her, but would he really care if she was here for herself or for her mother? She doubted it. And what was this about money? Since when were small town veterinarians wealthy? She added, "Dr. Reed has money?"

"You know he does. Loads of it."

"How?"

"Wise investments, his wife's estate. Don't act dumb with me, Lora."

There was no denying that money was nice and that it would relieve a lot worries, but money had nothing to do with love. Besides, due to her own resourcefulness, they would soon have a tidy influx of cash. Why else did she have that greenhouse and why else had she been slaving away during every spare moment? Unsure how to handle this situation, she started out by saying, "You're wrong about me."

"I checked the facts—"

"Okay, not wrong about everything, just about my motives."

"Then explain yourself."

"No."

He looked surprised. Running a hand through his hair, he regarded her steadily until he finally said, "No?"

"No. I don't see any reason why I should explain myself to you. I'm exactly who I say I am. My name is Lora Gifford. I work with my mom and grandma at our family florist shop. Okay, I borrowed Boggle from my neighbor and I made up a phone number but that's because you wouldn't stop flirting with me and I've recently sworn off men."

His brow narrowed. "I did not flirt with you," he said.

"Oh, come off it. You wanted my phone number."

"I told you, that's office protocol."

"Give me a break. I've been flirted with by real pros. I know when a man is coming on to me."

He sank down onto the bench and stared up at her. "Lora Gifford, you're either an amazingly talented dissembler or you're endowed with thought processes I can't begin to comprehend. I honestly don't know which it is. I'm not sure it matters."

She felt a smile threatening. She tried to nip it in the bud—it seemed an inappropriate time to smile—but she just couldn't help herself. She was dying to tell him all about her plot to unite Dr. Reed and her mother and share a good laugh, but he'd sworn he'd tell Dr. Reed everything she said, so how could she? Everyone knew that once something like that was common knowledge, the game was as good as over, and she truly did like Victor Reed. In fact, she'd set her sights on him and nothing was going to ruin it.

Jon frowned at her smile.

She sat beside him. "I wouldn't hurt or take advantage of Dr. Reed any more than you would," she said. Sitting so close had been a miscalculation on her part. She hadn't realized how short the benches were, how close they would be forced to sit, how his thigh and shoulder would brush against hers. She wanted to move away, but as she was trying to elicit his trust, suddenly jumping to her feet seemed counterproductive. She stayed put and tried to think clearly.

"I know my actions seem squirrely," she said, now aware of his body heat permeating the two layers of cloth separating their skin. "I know I've lied to you, but I genuinely like Dr. Reed and I have no desire to take advantage of him in any way. I didn't know he had money, it doesn't matter. I don't want his house or anything else."

That little voice piped up in the back of her head again. *How about his partner? Do you want him?*

No! she told her libido.

"I wish I could believe you," he said.

"Dr. Reed and I kind of connected at the hospital. He knew my dad. I'm not trying to seduce him, that's silly. I just want to get to know him. Is that so hard to understand?"

"That's all very nice," he said, staring right into her eyes, "but it doesn't explain why you came into the office to meet him in the first place, does it?"

"You're not going to give an inch, are you?"

"Not when it concerns Victor."

Standing abruptly, she said, "You have nothing to tell Dr. Reed about me except for some vague, unfounded suspicions and the fact that I commandeered a cat and was embarrassed to admit I brought the flowers myself as an excuse to meet him. Dr. Reed is paying me to stay here and I need the money to fix the van. So back off and leave me alone."

"Then you are here for money."

"It's a job."

"I'll pay you what he said he'd pay you if you leave right now."

"No, thanks, I actually like to work for my money. Why don't you go back to your own place?"

"No way," he said. Standing, he added, "This is a warning. I plan to stay here as long as you do. Someone has to look out for Victor's interests. I'm going to watch every step you take."

She shrugged. "Maybe I'll keep an eye on you to make sure you're as noble as you say you are."

Eyes flashing, he said, "I'm not noble, I just know when someone is not who they appear to be."

She shook her head and walked back toward the house, aware she should be unnerved by his threat, feeling a shimmery thrill instead.

He was going to keep an eye on her, hmm? That should be interesting.

Okay, so she'd sworn off men.

That didn't mean she couldn't drive one remarkably irritating specimen a little crazy—strictly on his own terms—did it?

She added a swish to her walk.

Take that!

Chapter Three

"May I help you?"

Jon Woods closed the glass door behind him and turned to find an older woman with flyaway white hair and robin egg-blue eyes.

Smoothing her hands over a yellow apron emblazoned with the words Lora Dunes Florist, she tilted her head and regarded him. Seldom had he been studied with quite so diligent a gaze. He felt she was taking in and recording every inch of his six feet, every one of his one hundred and seventy-five pounds, every brownish hair on his head.

"I need flowers," he said.

She smiled brilliantly. "You've come to the right place. Oh, unless you need them arranged because I'm all alone here and not very good at actually making fancy arrangements. Now, for that, young man, you need to see my daughter or better yet, my granddaughter. Lora is a whiz with flowers, it's in her blood. Why she could make a handful of weeds look like a million bucks." She glanced at her watch and added, "She should be back from midday deliveries in about an hour. I could fetch you some nice iced tea while you wait...."

Her voice trailed off expectantly. He couldn't help but smile. The woman had said everything so fast she was now a tad breathless.

He said, "I just want some flowers."

"This way to the cooler," she said over her shoulder. "Is this for your *wife?*"

"For a friend," he said firmly.

The older woman stopped in front of a refrigerated glass case in which resided dozens and dozens of flowers of all shapes, colors, sizes. He'd never seen so many flowers in one place at one time. "Do you actually send these *specific* flowers all the way to Los Angeles?"

"Oh, no. I'm sorry, I didn't understand. You want to send flowers?"

"Yes."

"Then you need to come check out our book. We fax your order to a florist down there."

He stared at the huge book she offered. No way was he going to flip through all of that. "How about a dozen white roses. Long stems. In a box," he said.

"Excellent choice," the woman said as she retrieved an order form.

As he took a platinum charge card out of his wallet, he said, "It must be nice working alongside your granddaughter."

The woman studied the card for a second. "Lora is such a dear. And so pretty! It's hard to believe she's still unmarried. Of course, that former fiancé of hers is to blame."

A fiancé? Hadn't Lora mentioned she'd recently sworn off men? So, she'd been jilted, that's why she was so touchy. Jilted by a young man, setting her sights on an older one, huh? At odds with the dating scene? Well she'd been mistaken if she thought she could take a shortcut to marriage by trapping Victor. He said, "Are you saying she doesn't date?"

"Calvin broke her heart, but she'll mend when the right man comes along. You watch!"

He said, "I think I may have seen your granddaughter around. She's very pretty." He finally noticed a name tag pinned to the woman's apron. *Ella.*

"Looks just like her mother and her great-grandmother. The looks skipped my generation. I look like my grandfather."

"You sell yourself short," he said.

She all but blushed. "So, it must be a pretty special lady you're sending these roses to. Your mother, maybe?" This innocent question was accompanied by a swift upward glance from the corners of her blue eyes.

Without smiling at the transparency of the conversation, he said, "No. Now, about Lora—"

"Maybe if I put in a good word, she'll go out with you. After all, you're not a teenager, are you?"

"Not for a long time now."

"Good. Lora is a dear. So many plans...not that she isn't getting ready to settle down. She would have married that no-account Calvin if he hadn't left her like he did. I think a woman, even in this day and age of liberation, needs a man to take care of her. What do you think?"

"I'm not sure," he said.

He'd obviously given the wrong answer. Ella made a deep sound in her throat before demanding, "Are you one of those men who think a woman should work all day as well as have the babies and care for the home?"

He tried a smile and a shrug and a noncommittal, "I suppose it depends on what the woman wants."

"Humph—" she said, handing him back his credit card.

He got the distinct feeling he'd fallen from her graces, which meant she might clam up so he added, "Of course, I hope when I marry that my wife will be content with a more traditional role.'' He almost choked on these words. Trina's idea of cleaning a house was hiring a maid.

Warmth flooded the older woman's smile. "That's a beautiful jacket you're wearing. The fabric is gorgeous. Cashmere? I bet you didn't purchase it in our little town. It's too pricey for Fern Glen.''

It *was* a pricey jacket. He'd bought it the winter before. He'd bought it because Trina liked him in good clothes.

Truth was, Trina liked all sorts of good things. They'd met when she brought her aging dog into the office because of a cough. Turned out the dog was allergic to cigarette smoke and Trina's boyfriend smoked. So much for the boyfriend. Once Trina had made sure Jon didn't have any habits that might annoy her pup, she'd whirled into his life like a tornado through a trailer park.

Not that he'd minded. Trina was a looker with a very suggestive walk and a sultry laugh. She'd introduced him to all her friends, invited him to countless Hollywood parties. She'd secured dozens of new patients for him, mostly women, all obsessed with their pets to one degree or another. He'd heard himself called the ''vet to the stars,'' a nickname that was good for business but made him squirm. He was learning to live with it, however, and there was no doubt that life with Trina was exhilarating. He'd been about to suggest she move in with him when his dad died.

"Must take a good job to afford such classy clothes,'' Ella said.

He regarded her with new misgivings. Why was she going on like this? Was it money she was after or was it a boyfriend for her granddaughter? Or both? Had he been right about Lora's motives?

For an instant he was disappointed. He didn't want to be right. There was something so fresh and breezy about Lora Gifford—he'd never really met anyone quite like her. Open one moment, closed the next, fabricating details right before his eyes, biting her lip as she apparently fought her conscience when telling them.

And her looks. She was an eyeful but not in the Trina way. Lora was something of a waif, casual about her appearance, scrubbed clean and tantalizingly wholesome, but mismatched and dwarfed within her sweater and jeans.

And yet alluring, somehow.

As a matter of fact, out in that gazebo, he'd had to remind himself he wasn't interested in her as a woman. There had been a couple of times when she'd looked at him and he'd felt his heart skip around. Was she right, had he flirted with her in his office without even knowing he was doing so?

Tonight he would call Trina and insist she venture north for a visit. He was under no illusion that she would find this remote coastline any more invigorating than he did, but if she cared for him, she would surely find time to come brighten his volunteer exile, wouldn't she?

Back to Lora. What would make her zero in on Victor? She'd never met the man before yesterday, so why him? Was it that friend of hers, the one with the Irish Setter? Had the friend gone on and on about the friendly, kind, *rich* old vet? But what drove Lora to implement such a plan?

She must need money. He looked around the threadbare shop and suddenly thought he understood. He said, "This is a nice place you have."

"It belonged to my daughter and her husband until the bum had a midlife crisis and left my Angela holding the bag," Ella said. She pushed across the form so he could fill in the delivery details. Lowering her voice, she confided, "But Lora assured us everything will be fine, she'll make sure the shop survives. Lora has a plan."

"A plan?"

Ella smiled. "A plan. She won't discuss it, it's a big

secret, but she says if things work out right, everything will be okay.''

There it was, more or less in writing. Lora's plan to guarantee the survival of her family's shop was simple: *marry Victor.*

''So what do you do for a living?'' Ella asked.

''I'm a vet.''

''My brother was in the army, fought in Korea. The war didn't kill him, but a two pack a day habit did.''

''No, I mean a doctor—''

She interrupted him with a squeal. ''A doctor? How wonderful.''

''Well, of sorts. Actually—''

She interrupted him again. ''How about taking out a contract to have fresh flowers delivered to your office every week? Lots of professionals do it. Flowers make your practice look very affluent.''

''Sure,'' he said, surprising himself. Maybe he was tired of trying to get a word in edgewise. Maybe he thought that by taking out this contract, he'd stay connected and could keep his eye on things even after Lora moved out. *If* Lora moved out.

Hell, maybe he was just nuts.

Once he'd agreed, the wheels of commerce turned amazingly fast, and he left a little bit later having agreed to a year of flowers. He knew he'd have to pay for them out of his own pocket—how could he ask Victor to support such a silly thing?

As he slid into his Porsche, he reviewed what he'd learned about Lora. Some guy named Calvin had jilted her, she'd promised her family she'd take care of them, the shop was foundering.

Why did it feel so hollow to be so right?

That night he offered to do the dishes. Lora had made vegetable lasagna with a béchamel sauce for dinner and

Victor was right—she could cook. She'd carted all the food into the den so Victor wouldn't have to get out of his recliner, set the low coffee table with fresh pink flowers she said she'd found while poking around in Victor's weed patch and entertained the older man with elaborate stories that all seemed to revolve around her mother, Angela, who was coming to weed the next day.

Jon, however, had refused to be entertained by this beguiling tease, preferring instead to study her in order to discern how she was going about her seduction. She didn't touch Victor, she didn't gaze into his eyes, she didn't talk about herself. Her methods were a mystery to him but there was no doubt that Victor was enchanted with her, so whatever her scheme was, it seemed to be working.

And the way she looked tonight! As he scrubbed the casserole dish, he thought about her. She'd changed from jeans and baggy sweater to a dress, a gauzy greenish blue one that seemed to have a little aqua colored slip beneath it that came down longer on her legs than the dress itself and which managed to look innocent and naughty at one and the same time. Her eyes, because of the dress, appeared greener than ever. With her wavy black hair framing her gamin face and trailing down her back in luscious handfuls, and that dress skimming her slender body, the tiny straps slipping down her arm every once in a while and tossed back in place with a gesture so casual it had to be planned, he'd found it hard not to gawk. It was a relief to take sanctuary in the kitchen.

He needed to call Trina.

"Need help?"

Her voice came from behind him and he purposely didn't turn around. "No, thanks," he called and scrubbed harder.

"I'll dry," she said, coming to his side, a fresh dish towel in hand.

He said nothing. Maybe she would take the hint and go away.

She lifted a plate from the strainer and began polishing it. "Imagine my surprise," she said conversationally, "when I got back to the shop this afternoon and discovered my grandmother had talked you into twelve months of flowers. That's fifty-two arrangements. And she got you to sign a contract, something none of our other customers would even consider. Seems that Mom and I have seriously underestimated Gram's sales ability. I think a promotion is in order."

"I didn't have to sign a contract?" he asked, looking at her for the first time since dinner. Mistake. The color of her eyes was subdued in this light but that did nothing to detract from their glimmering allure. He looked away.

"Of course not."

"She didn't mention that."

"Kind of like you didn't mention knowing me? Well, that's the price of snooping."

"I wasn't snooping, I needed flowers."

"A dozen white roses, no less. Grandma admitted she couldn't get you to tell her who you were sending them to. Just a woman named Trina Odell in Beverly Hills."

"Your grandmother is amazing."

"Isn't she?" Lora picked up another plate. "Why aren't you married?" she added. "Mind you, I couldn't care less one way or another, but Grandma is afraid you might be a playboy and in her book, that's about the same thing as being a serial killer."

He half laughed. "Trust me, I'm not a playboy."

"How old are you?"

"Thirty-three."

"Kind of old to be single. I asked Dr. Reed and he said you've never been married. Why?"

"Now who's being a snoop?"

"You owe us. You came into the shop and asked all sorts of questions."

"Actually, with your grandmother, it isn't necessary to ask all sorts of questions. She volunteers a lot of information. Besides, I left my name on a contract you were likely to see, so I wasn't trying to be secretive."

"But you pumped my grandmother for information. That's kind of despicable."

"Feeling protective of her?"

"Of course."

"Now you know how I feel about Victor."

His gaze moved from her eyes to her lips and he felt a little jolt in his chest. Her lips! Why hadn't he noticed them before? They were perfectly plump and delectable. They reminded him of two succulent cherry candies and he found himself suddenly fighting one hell of a sweet tooth!

"Okay, point taken," she said.

He struggled to recall the topic of their conversation and was relieved when she fell silent. He went back to all but sand-blasting the casserole dish. He felt dazed.

He wanted to kiss her.

How ironic was that?

This was nuts, but the thought of tasting Lora's lips filled his head like one of those old television images of an exploding atom bomb, like a huge mushroom cloud blurring everything else. He recited Trina's phone number.

Squirting more dish soap into the sink, he scrubbed up a new batch of bubbles which immediately caused his nose to itch. He glanced at his sudsy hands, wrinkled his nose, tried to rub his face against his own shoulder. Nothing worked. He was just about to dry his hands and take care of it properly when she said, "Where does it itch?"

"The left side, but you don't—"

"No problem," she said, reaching up and gently touching the side of his nose. Her fingers felt warm, her caress gentle. Was it his imagination or did her fingertips linger a bit? Her gaze met his and she smiled as she dropped her hand.

"So," she said after a few moments, "why haven't you ever married? No, don't tell me, let me take a guess. It's this Trina woman, right, the one from Beverly Hills? Bleached hair, long legs." Holding her hands way out in front of her chest, she added, "Boobs out to here."

He laughed. "More or less."

"Is that where you're from?"

"Beverly Hills? Yes."

"So you and Trina have been dating for a while."

"Two years."

"And now she wants a condo in the sky and pretty little blond babies of her own. You panicked and moved away and now you're sending her flowers because you know that was a cowardly thing to do."

"You're getting cold," he said, wondering why Lora seemed suddenly angry with him. "Icy," he added. "Brr—"

"Okay, you're the one who got serious. She told you to get lost and you moved here and now you're trying to woo her back with flowers."

"There's no problem with our relationship," he said firmly.

"Really? Then why did you move so far away from her? That's screwy."

"I didn't. I don't live here, Lora. I'm just filling in for Victor for a couple of months. Didn't you know that?"

He could see by the expression on her face that she had assumed he lived in Fern Glen. She fell silent for a moment, something that should have relieved him but didn't. He finally said, "Besides, Trina wouldn't dream of living up here."

"What's she got against Fern Glen?"

"Let's just say that Trina is a big city girl."

"Meaning there's not enough happening in Fern Glen to amuse her."

"Exactly. And of course she has a broad circle of friends down there and a good job working at one of the big studios and dreams of making it in the movies."

"Does she stand a chance?"

"Of course."

"And you?"

"No movie star ambitions. I'm a veterinarian down there just as I am up here. I have a great practice and two terrific partners."

"You must miss your girlfriend."

"Yes. I'm thinking I can coax her north for a short visit. Two and a half months is a long time to be apart."

"You think she'll like it here?"

"Maybe."

"I've known women like your Trina," Lora said abruptly. "She isn't going to be impressed by community theater, foggy beaches and thousands of redwood trees. The humidity will frizz her hair into a fuzz ball. She'll hate it."

He bristled at her know-it-all attitude. "You don't know Trina. She's a good sport."

"Are you going to marry her?"

"Wait just a second," he protested. "Not only is that none of your business, but it's *really* none of your business." He said it with a smile, determined not to reveal the tight knot of tension that suddenly seized his gut. Marriage? Sure, he'd thought about it, a lot lately in his current lonely state, but to give that thought a voice? He needed to get control of this conversation again. He needed to wheedle from Lora more details about her diabolical get-Victor scheme.

"I'm sorry," she said softly, "you're right." After a few seconds, she added, "I've lived in Fern Glen my whole life."

He stared at her a second, avoiding her eyes and her lips, concentrating on her chin, which was cute but easier to resist than the other parts of her. Imagine living a whole lifetime in one small town located behind a curtain of giant trees, nestled against a cold ocean. Until his dad had moved here, he hadn't known the place existed and the thought of being a youngster here was daunting. He'd spent his youth in San Francisco, a cable car ride away from damn near anything.

As he finally surrendered the casserole dish, he said, "Turnaround is fair play. Why aren't you married?"

"I'm only twenty-four," she said. "I won't be twenty-five until June."

"Lots of women get married by almost twenty-five. I'm sure it's not as though you haven't had the opportunity."

She cast him a suspicious look. "I am *not* trying to hook Dr. Reed," she said impatiently.

He thought, *Sure you are, you little vixen,* but keeping his expression neutral, he said, "How about Calvin?"

Now she was rubbing the casserole dish with a vengeance. "Calvin Stuart?"

"The infamous ex."

Eyes wide, she said, "Grandma told you about Calvin?"

"Yes. And about your mother."

Lora sighed so deeply the fabric across her breasts stretched tight for a moment, hinting her petite figure might be curvier than he had imagined. That was the trouble, he was imagining way too much. He added, "I know your father…ran off. I guess a thing like that could kill a girl's faith in romance."

"My parents never should have married each other. They were like oil and water."

"So, why did they get married?"

"Because they were in love."

"But it didn't last."

"No, I guess it didn't. Do you think it's possible for love to last a lifetime?"

"I hope so," he said.

With a smile, she added, "My mother is a beautiful person inside and out. She's had some lousy times lately, but she still has hope. I admire that even if it's a little hard to understand. She deserves to be happy."

There was such a nostalgic tone to her voice that he surmised she was talking about herself, not her mom, then instantly chided himself for his cynicism. His own mother had died ten years before. There wasn't a doubt in his mind that had she survived, he'd be protective of her, especially now with his dad gone, and he reluctantly admired Lora's devotion.

"The flower shop must mean a lot to her," he said.

"I guess it's her whole life now."

"Your grandmother said you have a secret plan for the place."

"My grandmother, the chatterbox," Lora said with another sigh, but also with a fond smile on her full lips.

"I guess we both know what your plan is," he added.

With a defiant toss of her head that made her dark hair catch and hold a million dazzling threads of light, she corrected him. "I *know* what my plan is, you only *think* you know. It's not the same thing."

He gave up. "So tell me the truth about Calvin."

She shrugged again, her movement so graphic she didn't need words. The movement caused a black lingerie strap to slip down her shoulder and she ignored it. He fought the desire to flip it back into place as he said, "Come on, convince me the dolt didn't sour you on young love."

"Please, we were hardly Romeo and Juliet." She tucked the casserole dish in the cupboard, then draped the damp towel over the oven handle. Looking up at him, she smiled smugly and said, "I don't have to convince you of anything, remember? Take me as you find me, I'm an open book.''

"Ha.''

She bit at her lip for a second, then spared him a quick glance. "I need to ask you a favor," she said softly.

"I shudder to think.''

"For some reason my grandmother has taken a shining to you.''

"I wore my good jacket today plus I graciously signed a bogus contract for flowers I didn't need," he said. "No wonder she likes me. Plus, she thinks I'm a medical doctor.''

"I know she does.''

"It's not my fault. I tried to clear it up.''

"Trust me, I understand. Listen, I know you have a thing going with Trina and I would be the last woman on earth to ask you to betray her, so this is strictly on the up and up in a kind of underhanded way.''

He didn't have to pretend to be confused. Making sure his gaze didn't stay focused on that errant little strap, he warily said, "Go on.''

"Could you make a point of coming into the shop while I'm there?''

"I don't—''

"Just come into the shop during your lunch hour sometime next week. Call me 'honey' or mention a dinner date. Hopefully, Grandma will set her sights on you and stop trying to match me up with anyone and everyone. And since you and I know there is nothing between us, I will be off the hook and free to concentrate on more important things.'' She fidgeted with her dress for a second and added, "You know what? It wouldn't hurt if Mom was around to see this. She has her sights set on the guy across the street.''

"What's wrong with the guy across the street?''

"I don't suppose there's anything wrong with him, I've

never actually met the man. It's just that I'm tired of their games and if they think that you and I are—''

''Interested in one another?''

''That's the idea. That should get them off my back. They'll think you're quite a catch no matter what kind of doctor you are.''

As he thought, she finally fixed her strap. It was on the tip of his tongue to ask if he was as prime a catch as Victor, but he kept his mouth closed. This request of hers was interesting and he needed time to figure out if she was being completely up front about it. Was it possible her relatives didn't know about her plans to snag a wealthy husband? Off the top of his head, he couldn't see a hidden motive, but who knew?

Wait a second, did she simply want to take herself out of circulation so she could concentrate on Victor? But if Victor thought that he, Jon, and Lora were interested in each other, then wouldn't Victor back away from the perilous edge of the precipice called *Lora?* Maybe Jon could turn this to his advantage. He said, ''Why not?''

A relieved swallow was followed by another unexpected move on her part. Placing her hands on top of his shoulders, she raised herself on tiptoes and kissed his mouth. Her lips were soft and warm and her perfumed closeness enveloped him in such a sweet haze that he almost put his arms around her waist.

Within the blink of an eye, she was a foot away. ''Thanks. Good night, Jon.''

Despite the quirky streak that ran through her personality, he realized with dismay that he was sorry to see her leave. She hadn't given him any new information. She'd confirmed certain conclusions he'd reached, but he still had no idea how to discredit her to Victor.

Truth be known, she'd sidetracked him with that kiss. Her lips weren't candy, they were petals, soft and dewy.

And they were off limits.

So, which was she: sweetheart or con artist?

Or both…

Chapter Four

Lora closed her bedroom door and leaned back against it. That kiss had really jolted Jon!

The smile on her lips faded as she realized that it had also jolted her. Who would have guessed the man's lips would be that warm and soft or that his gaze would pierce her like a dart or that she would feel an overwhelming desire to tarry until he had a chance to put his hands around her waist? Because unless she'd forgotten everything she'd ever known about kissing, that was what he'd been about to do when she fled the room.

She unzipped her dress and flung it over a chair, pulled on a knee-length T-shirt and went into the little guest bath so conveniently attached to her room. She brushed her teeth furiously, trying to recall when she'd decided it would be a good idea to ask Jon to pretend to date her.

She knew exactly when. He'd been asking about why Calvin left and then tried to nose into her parents' failed relationship and then he'd gone back to quizzing her about Calvin. Calvin, Calvin, Calvin!

She'd begun to feel as though there wasn't enough oxygen in the room, like she'd been stuffed headfirst into a sleeping bag, claustrophobia and despair closing in....

Maybe she wasn't over Calvin yet, maybe that was it. Maybe the dreams they'd spun together still lingered in her mind, a bittersweet reminder that in the end, Calvin had felt pursuing his Chicago plan more important than marrying her and building a life together in Fern Glen.

Or maybe the thought of having to be friendly to a continuing parade of potential Calvins was just too much.

Pretending to date Jon was safe. His heart was invested in Trina Odell. By the way, she thought, Trina needed to change her last name if she wanted to be a movie star. Odell just wasn't catchy. Maybe something lyrical like *Lacrosse.* Lacrosse was nice, it was some kind of sport that involved a stick so it should remind movie fans of health and vigor. Lora couldn't think of a single movie star with that name so it would also be unique.

Or maybe Trina was just waiting to change her name to Woods.

Lora could see the headline: Trina Woods, Wife Of Popular Beverly Hills Vet, Jon Woods, Wins Second Academy Award!

Lora buried her face in a towel.

What in the world was wrong with her?

"Buck up," she told herself.

Jon had been so glad to go along with her plan and she knew why. He thought by agreeing to counterfeit dating, he was actually diverting her from her sordid scheme to entrap a rich, older husband for herself. He was offering himself like a sacrificial lamb to protect Dr. Reed.

The man was so transparent.

As she snuggled under the covers, she suddenly wasn't sure she liked the way he thought of her as such an opportunist.

Well, so what? What did it matter what he thought of her?

The trouble was that Jon Woods was likable. His faithfulness to his girlfriend, his decency in dropping everything at home to come up here to help Dr. Reed in his time of need, even his determination to protect the older man from Lora, were admirable—if sometimes misguided—characteristics. Now, thanks to his suspicious nature where she was concerned, he was going to help Lora avoid the perils of the man-traps her mother and grandmother so gleefully set.

This was good.

Why was she whining? It wasn't necessary that Jon like or respect her. He'd be gone in a few weeks and she'd never see him again. All she needed from him were two things: he needed to stay out of her plans to match up her mom and Dr. Reed and he needed to ask her for a date in front of her relatives. Period.

Nothing she and Jon would engage in would have even a nodding acquaintance with reality. He knew or thought he knew where she was coming from. She was absolutely sure she understood him. They would act out a little infatuation and Gram and Mom would happily back off. Jon would think he was saving Dr. Reed, she would have the space to encourage romance between the mending veterinarian and her mother plus concentrate on her true make-money scheme. Everything would be dandy!

Another thought.

What about her dad? Was this plan to marry off her mother in some way disloyal to him?

Nope, he'd left of his own free will, he'd initiated the divorce, he'd even hinted in a letter that he was flying off to see someone new. Dad was out of the picture. Just to make sure, she'd call him and feel him out.

Lora closed her eyes, and to her horror, her mind immediately filled with images of Jon. The way the muscles in his arms bunched as he scrubbed that casserole dish, the way he looked at her as though he wanted to throw her over his shoulder and toss her out of the house. His irritation, his smile, his voice, his strong hands…

Her eyes flew open and she stared into the dark.

"Careful," she whispered to herself, determined now that there would be no more kissing, not ever.

It's okay to light a match as long as you're careful not to start a fire….

Lora's mother showed up the next day with Grandma in tow, both of them wearing gardening clothes. In her mother's case, this was an excellent choice, as she wore midcalf khakis and a white sweater draped around her shoulders with her typical aplomb. Martha Stewart, look out!

Gram, on the other hand, wearing a blue T-shirt, yellow jacket, red knee-length shorts and white tennis shoes, resembled a talkative, friendly, dearly loved beach ball.

The two older women took charge of the weed patch and by the time Lora set out lunch and helped Dr. Reed hobble out to a lounge chair, they had the majority of the weeding done and were discussing vegetable gardening.

"Lora has this big greenhouse out back of her house but she keeps it locked and won't even let us inside," Lora's mom told Dr. Reed as she poured lemonade. "We could grow such tomatoes out there!"

Gram, assembling a sandwich from a platter of cold cuts, made her famous tsking sound. "And she won't tell us what she does out there every morning and half the weekend."

"Perhaps she's hiding from us," her mother said with a knowing glance at Lora.

"Or growing marijuana," Gram said, pronouncing it "marry-juana." She added a pickle to her plate.

Dr. Reed regarded Lora with raised eyebrows. Lora smiled and shook her head.

"Her father was much the same," Angela Gifford said. "George always had a project going. Remember, Lora?"

What was her mother doing bringing up her father? *No, no, no!* "No," Lora said fiercely.

"Yes, you do. Tying fish lures or working on outboard motors…it was always something with that man."

"Did Lora tell you I used to fish with your husband?" Dr. Reed said.

Her mother beamed.

Lora said, "Her ex-husband."

"Not technically, not for a month," her mother said.

Lora felt herself gaping. She hadn't known there was still a month to go.

Her mother added, "Lora never told me you knew George. It must have slipped her mind. How about that?"

"Well, I believe you would have to say that I *knew* George as in the past tense. Time was we'd meet out on the North Jetty, me with my boys, George in a crazy red hat."

"His lucky hat," Angela Gifford said. "I gave it to him."

"I recall seeing Lora a few times and you, too."

"George loved to fish. Just loved it."

When was her mother going to stop! Lora felt like gagging her. She sent a mental image to her mother: *Eat something and shut up!*

Dr. Reed said, "He loved it because he *always* seemed to catch a bigger fish than me."

Angela laughed fondly. *Fondly!* She said, "He's a pretty good cook, too. He taught me how to barbecue salmon. George always has such high energy."

Lora wanted to slap a hand over her mother's mouth. Thankfully, Gram came to the rescue.

"He had enough energy to walk out on you, that's for sure, and he didn't look back once. Now Vic," Gram added as though she'd already accepted Dr. Reed as promising son-in-law material, ''I keep thinking that weed patch of yours would make a perfect veggie garden.''

''I recall my late wife used it for exactly that purpose,'' Dr. Reed said as he accepted a plate piled high with food from Lora's mother. Was it Lora's imagination or did Dr. Reed's fingers graze her mother's hand and did her mother look away to hide a smile?

At just that moment, Jon came through the sliding doors, all three dogs and the white cat gamboling about his feet. It was a lovely spring day, one of the few so far north and close to the ocean that hadn't come with fog, wind or rain. The sun shining through the trees dappled his dark hair with pale light. He was dressed in jeans and a red T-shirt. The memory of the rock-solid feel of his chest caught Lora unaware and she blinked rapidly.

''Come build yourself a sandwich,'' Dr. Reed called.

Jon looked at the small gathering and signaled that he'd join them soon. As he stooped to pick up the cat, Dr. Reed said, ''Look at the way he handles animals. I tell you, the boy has a way with them.''

''He's awfully good-looking,'' Gram said with a glance at Lora who studiously began piling shredded carrots onto a roll. ''I think you could classify him as a hunk.''

Dr. Reed chuckled. ''I guess he takes after his dad in that department, though you ladies would know more about that kind of thing than I would. Doug was my partner for fifteen years before his heart gave out, but as good as Doug was with small animals, Jon is better. He talks to them in a real soothing voice. It must inspire confidence. No wonder he's such a hit with the pampered pets of the rich and famous down there in L.A. He even makes house calls, if you can believe it.''

''You mean he's not a people doctor?'' Gram asked.

''Nope. Neither am I, Elloise.''

Elloise? Lora hadn't heard anyone use her grand-mother's formal name in quite a while. It sounded nice, but she doubted it would curb her grandmother's tendency to speak her mind and in this instance, that would probably have something to do with Jon not being a "real" doctor.

"Treating God's little critters is an honorable thing to do," Gram said unexpectedly. "I can't imagine why he ordered flowers for a veterinarian's office, though. Well, no matter, they'll brighten the place up."

Lora took her haphazardly piled plate and sank down onto a bench, her appetite gone, her mind a maelstrom. Was it just her or did the conversation that day have a surreal quality about it? And what about Jon? She sneaked a peak at him and sighed.

Why couldn't he look like a toad? Why did he have to walk that way and why did he have to have such a nice smile? Sick animals didn't care what he looked like, only silly human females cared about such superficial things.

Dr. Reed cleared his throat and added, "It's a shame Jon won't stay up here in Fern Glen. This community could use a man like him. I hate to see him leave."

Lora could barely wait to see him go. Tomorrow wouldn't be too soon. Today would be better. He confused her.

As Jon claimed the seat beside hers, the animals spread out to beg, sniff and flop down on the grass. The three older people segued back into garden talk. Lora stared at her makeshift sandwich and had a sudden and intense desire to go fool around in her greenhouse, by herself, away from everyone and everything.

"I saw you ogling Victor," Jon said out the side of his mouth.

She turned abruptly to face him. He was smiling. Darn that smile. She whispered, "Honestly, you have an incredible imagination."

"*I* have an incredible imagination? Well, coming from you, I guess that's a compliment. By the way, your mother is an attractive woman, isn't she?"

"Yes," Lora said, studying his face for signs that he had finally tumbled upon the true nature of her plan.

"She and Victor seem to be engaged in some kind of dialogue."

Lora turned. Sure enough, her mom and Dr. Reed were face-to-face, lips moving, hands gesturing as they apparently discussed the superiority of this cold weather crop over that one. What was with her mother? Why in the world was she arguing with Dr. Reed over broccoli? Did she argue with every man?

Shudder—here was a thought. Was it possible her father wasn't totally at fault for the years of family tension?

Meanwhile, the smaller dog, Bow Wow, had discovered that Gram was a soft touch and now lurked by her knees, waiting for bits of ham and peppered turkey to materialize in her outstretched fingers.

"Your grandmother is a doll," Jon said suddenly.

Lora smiled as she looked at her grandmother and silently agreed. "I think she misses Grandpa," she heard herself say.

Jon said, "I know my father never got over losing my mother. Some people just seem to be made for each other, don't they?"

"Are you thinking of you and Trina?"

"Are you thinking of you and Victor?"

She turned to face him. "You never give up."

"Me!"

"Anyway, I think Grandma could fall in love again."

"Have anyone in mind?"

"There's a very dapper man who buys flowers for his mother every Monday afternoon. Henry Mitchell is his name. I think he kind of likes Grandma. She says he has too many freckles on his bald head. Apparently that's a turn-off for her. And there's another gentleman who peers in the shop window on his way to and from the bakery."

"You think he's lusting for your grandmother through the glass?"

"Either that or Gram decided I should hook up with a seventy-year-old retired librarian and he's checking *me* out."

"You have a thing for older men, don't you?" he said.

Frowning, she said, "Enough already!"

"So, about our big date."

Lora shrugged her shoulders. "Next week you can come into the shop—"

"What about right now? Everyone is here. Or don't you want Victor to know you're dating me?"

"I'm not dating you."

"Pretending to date me, then."

"I don't care if Dr. Reed knows."

"Right." He caught a spiral of her hair and curled it around his finger.

"What are you doing?" she whispered.

"Setting the stage. Pretending to look enamored."

She tried to pull away. "Well, stop it!"

"Oh, come on now. Maybe Victor will get jealous. You'd like that, wouldn't you?"

"Jon, I'm about ready to dump a glass of lemonade in your lap."

"Come on. Didn't that little kiss last night give you ideas? I know it got me to thinking." Without waiting for a response, he planted his lips on hers.

From the corners of her eyes, Lora could see the other three people in the yard staring at them. She felt her face burn. She wanted to yell, "This is not what you think. This is…nothing!"

"I'll go get more…bread…." she stammered instead, pushing herself away from Jon and the amused gleam in his eyes.

"Yikes," she mumbled once inside the house, rubbing

her lips with the back of her hand and trying desperately to remember what she'd said she'd come inside to fetch.

The man had just called her bluff.

The game was afoot.

She grabbed her car keys and left.

Jon gently rubbed the orange and white ears of his current patient. She was a sweet little calico with green eyes and a ballooned figure that would definitely keep her off the cover of *Cat Beauty* magazine.

Her owner, in contrast, was a striking brunette with almond-shaped eyes. "This cat is a stray," she explained. "My husband insists on feeding it. It's all bloated like it has a tumor. I think you should put it out of its misery."

"She doesn't have a tumor," Jon said patiently.

"Then what's wrong with her?"

"She's pregnant," he explained. "Very pregnant." He looked in the animal's mouth and added, "This is a young cat, not even a year old." The cat rubbed his finger and he smiled at her. She had a pretty little face and snowy whiskers.

The woman groaned. "Kittens? How many?"

Jon looked at the woman as the calico purred and licked the back of his hand. "I don't know."

"Can't you tell?"

"No, I can't. But I'd say she's very close to giving birth. Let's see, a cat's gestation period is about nine weeks. Did you happen to notice when she started 'looking funny' to you or when her nipples started to redden—"

"I never look at her!" the woman interrupted. "I told you, she's a stray."

"Okay. Well, I advise you to take her home and fix up a cardboard box with some clean newspaper in it. Destroy the box after birthing and set her up with a new box—"

"I don't want kittens," the woman interrupted again.

Jon stared at her. "It's kind of late—"

"She's a stray. I keep telling you that."

Jon finally noticed that the woman hadn't once touched the animal since he'd lifted the little creature from the cardboard box carrier. She hadn't even looked at it and now she was actually backing away. "I don't want the cat, either."

"But your husband—"

"I don't like cats. Give it to someone else."

He half smiled as he said, "You'd be surprised how few people want a pregnant stray cat."

"I don't care. I don't want kittens." And with that, she turned on her heels and walked out of the office.

Jon waited a second for her to return. Surely she would immediately regret her impulsive exit. He gazed at the crack in the wall and the faded poster showing breeds of dogs. From the back of the building, he could hear a dog wailing and a Siamese cat howling like crazy. Where was that woman? He finally picked up the little calico and held her against his chest. As he burst through the door, Connie, the assistant, turned to face him.

"Mrs. Pullman left in a hurry," Connie said. "What's wrong?"

"She's gone?"

"Long gone. In fact, I've never seen anyone move that fast in that high a heel. What happened?"

He handed Connie the calico. "Mrs. Pullman had a meltdown. Find the kitty a nice warm spot in the back, will you? Then try to call *Mr.* Pullman for me."

Connie took the cat and Jon returned to the exam room, picked up the file and opened the opposite door leading to the long area that ran in back of all three examination rooms and functioned as a lab and work space. Another door off of this one led to the surgery, but he made his way to Victor's office, climbing over bags of dry dog food and a hundred other veterinary related items that cluttered the small space.

His father's office across the hall had been turned into storage after his dad's death, but the overflow still piled up in every hallway, in every crevice. Jon didn't know why Victor hadn't replaced his dad, he didn't know how Victor handled the workload by himself, he could only speculate that Victor was nearing the time he would retire and didn't want to invest any more energy into this operation.

But it was a nice little place, staffed with competent, decent, animal-loving people, situated on a quiet road with available land for expansion, the potential for growth evident by the new housing going up nearby. It needed updating, but even that was doable. However, Victor must have his reasons for keeping things as they were, and heaven knew Jon didn't want to get any more involved than he was already.

He made a few notes in the Pullman file, looked at the schedule and found that the remainder of the afternoon was clear. Well, what was left of the afternoon as it was already well after five o'clock.

Connie stuck her head in the door. "These just came. There was no card but the florist said you'd understand. What do you want me to do with them?" she asked, her arms full of flowers.

Jon laughed. It looked as though his monthly delivery of flowers had just commenced. "Take them home and enjoy them," he said.

"Really? Gee, thanks. And I called Mr. Pullman but he wasn't home so I called his store and the guy there said Pullman was off on a business trip down in Santa Rosa and wouldn't be back 'til the end of the week."

Jon swallowed a sigh. "What do you mean 'store'? The Pullman's have a store of some kind?"

"They own the wine shop on the plaza."

Jon vaguely recalled seeing it. If memory served him

right, the place was a few doors down from Lora's flower shop.

Connie added, "What do you want me to do?"

"Nothing. I guess we'll have to wait until the husband gets home or the wife comes to her senses. Maybe I'll stop by the store and talk to her."

"Don't wait too long," Connie said, her expelled breath causing a fern frond to flutter. A fern that Lora had undoubtedly tucked into place, that she had touched with her fingers. "That little kitty is about to burst," Connie warned.

I've got to get out of here, Jon thought suddenly, scattering a pile of drug company samples as he abruptly popped to his feet. But where? The thought of going home to Victor's house didn't thrill him.

She'd be there.

It wasn't that he didn't want to see her—it was that he wanted to see her too much.

She was like that, sneaky, ingratiating herself without him even knowing how she did it. Like getting him to kiss her in front of everyone.

Okay, he'd come up with that brilliant idea all by himself. He'd thought he'd give her a taste of her own medicine. If it had backfired, then he alone had to shoulder the blame. Who would have guessed that a second quick kiss would leave him with this burning and illogical desire for another?

He was homesick, that was it, and trying to keep Lora from taking advantage of Victor meant that he had to think about her all the time and try to outguess her. He'd wanted to unsettle her by kissing her in front of Victor; he'd wanted Victor to get the idea that he was smitten with the little charlatan. It had seemed like the most expedient way to protect his father's old friend.

Then Lora flew out of there as though a saber-toothed tiger was after her and though Victor's smile had to mean he'd seen them kiss and had drawn conclusions that should safeguard him, Jon felt like a fool.

No way he was going straight to Victor's house.

What he needed to do was take a walk or jog or do something to ease the restlessness that churned in his gut. He changed into running shoes and grabbed a jacket, glad when the door to the office closed behind him.

The Porsche tore up the miles to Clam Beach. He parked beside a black truck old enough to have voted in the 1988 presidential election and locked his car. The hike across the dunes felt good, and once he hit the miles of exposed flat sand, he took off at a good pace and ran beside the pounding surf until a creek bisecting the beach halted his progress. Then he turned around and ran back the way he'd come.

The sun was plunging toward the horizon and he stood facing the surf for some time, cooling off, watching the relentless beat of the ocean as the quickening breeze blew bits of foam and seaweed along the sand. Way down the beach, he could see a big black dog fetching sticks for a bundled figure. It made him want a dog of his own, an urge he'd resisted so far because of the condo in which he lived. Maybe it was time to buy a house with a decent yard. Did such a thing exist in Beverly Hills in his price range?

That's how it was up here, though. One person on the beach, besides him, and one dog. A few dozen seagulls. Everything here was so…well, stark. At home, this beach would be crawling with people craving a glimpse of the ocean, a dip in the surf, a good run or an idle walk. But here, with a population just a fraction of what he was used to, the beach was all but empty.

He started back across the dunes with a new uneasiness growing in his chest, this one not so easy to name, or, he suspected, tame.

Everything was beautiful. Cold, windy, austere at times...and beautiful. And lonely.

In the back of his head, he heard Lora telling him Trina would hate it here, that the damp weather would frizz her hair. He smiled to himself as he tried to imagine Trina with frizzy hair. The woman always looked picture perfect, her platinum tresses slick and smooth. She was fond of saying that a person never knew who was looking at them and she had to be prepared in case she happened to walk into a movie director's line of vision.

Well, he imagined that despite Lora's comments, Trina would wrap a scarf around her hair and muddle through just fine. He decided that he would call Trina when he got back to Victor's house and encourage her to hop on a plane for a visit north. He still had his apartment, she could stay there. Hell, maybe he'd give up protecting Victor and stay with her! They could build a beach fire and cuddle by the embers, walk arm in arm on the firm sand and maybe this gnawing feeling in his gut would go away.

And then, maybe, he could stop thinking about Lora Gifford.

When he got back to the parking lot, he found a man standing by the old truck, a black and tan terrier sitting on the open gate. The dog had one paw raised and looked so much like Trina's dog, Bitsy, that Jon did a double take. One difference was obvious: Bitsy would never lower himself to raise his paw for a human. Jon finally noticed the way the dog recoiled every time his owner tried to touch him. Soft whimpers drifted on the breeze.

"Problem?" Jon asked as he slowly approached. The owner looked to be about his own age, almost as tall but decidedly unkempt with longish dark blond hair, a scraggly beard and loose-fitting, faded clothes that seemed to have been salvaged from a larger man. In contrast, the dog's coat had the glossy sheen of health.

"Bill got something stuck in his paw only he won't let

me touch it to help him,'' the man said, his voice so soft Jon had to strain to hear him.

"I'm pretty good with dogs," Jon said. "Mind if I try?"

"I don't know—"

"I'm a vet," Jon added.

The man delivered a quick glance and then a shy, "I'd appreciate your help."

Using deliberate but slow motions and talking in a low, comforting voice, Jon perched himself on the gate next to the dog. He put a hand on the animal's head and drew it slowly down the silky back. The dog perked his ears and stared at Jon as though thinking things over.

"What's wrong, Bill, you got a thorn in one of your pads?" Jon crooned as he started at the head again and this time ran a hand down the dog's good leg.

Bill didn't flinch.

Still talking nonsense to the dog, Jon ran his hand down the animal's chest and then onto the bad leg, inching toward the paw. The dog, still staring at Jon with soulful dark eyes, allowed Jon to touch the paw, to gently clutch it, to turn it in his hand.

Very softly, Jon said to the man standing behind him, "Do you have a flashlight?"

"No. I used to have one, but…"

Jon used his free hand to dig his keys out of his pocket and handed them to the stranger. "You'll find one in a black box tucked in the trunk. Bring the whole box. Move slowly though, let Bill keep track of you."

The man did as asked and the dog watched, still allowing Jon to hold the paw. It was impossible for Jon to tell if there was anything in the black pad—the light was too poor.

Eventually, the owner produced the box, and following Jon's directions, flooded the animal's paw with light. A sliver of sparkly glass imbedded in the pad explained everything. The owner followed directions as Jon told him which implement to hand over. Within a few seconds, the glass was out and Jon had disinfected the area. Bill bathed Jon's face in his enthusiasm.

"Bill likes you," the man said.

"He's a great dog. My name is Jon Woods, by the way. I'm filling in for Victor Reed at the Animal Clinic."

"Nolan Wylie," the man said, staring at the pavement. Addressing his comments to the taillight, he said, "Dr. Woods gave Bill his rabies shot last year. He was Dr. Reed's partner. I think he died."

"He was my dad," Jon said.

Nolan nodded solemnly. "I'm sorry. What do I owe you for helping me out today?"

"You don't owe me a thing," Jon said. "I'm happy I could help."

Nolan's gaze briefly met Jon's as he said, "I live right up the road. It's not much, but…well, if you want, you can follow me home. I brew my own beer…."

Jon, thinking about Victor's house, knowing that Lora was no doubt stir-frying something delicious with her loose hair waving around her shoulders and her trim body encased in that aqua dress, decided a beer sounded good and the company of a man his own age, even a shy man who looked as though a hot shower and a trip to the local barber might improve his appearance, sounded even better.

For tonight, Victor would just have to fight Lora off with his chopsticks.

"You're on," he said.

Chapter Five

Two hours later, Jon let himself into Victor's house. It was still early, he was hungry and the thought of seeing Lora wasn't nearly as scary as it had been earlier.

In fact, now the thought of seeing her aroused a tingle of anticipation. He wanted to tell her about Nolan and Bill and the old house the reticent man seemed to spend his life rebuilding, about the riotous flowers obscuring a rotting foundation and spilling from any and all containers big enough to hold dirt, about the shelves of books on wildflowers that covered most of one wall and the exquisite watercolor paintings the man created and sold at Saturday markets to keep himself in nails, paint and dog food.

She'd appreciate the details, he thought. She'd think the way Nolan structured his destructured life to be kind of quirky and charming—well, he thought she would.

Though her van was parked out front, Jon found the house dark and empty except for the two larger dogs and a few cats who greeted him with much tail wagging. At least the dogs wagged. The cats barely looked up from their naps, especially Frosty, the white one, but Frosty was deaf, so that was to be expected. Jon peeked into every room—all empty—finally opening the door leading from the kitchen to the garage and flicking on the light.

Victor's big white car was gone.

Jon felt oddly deflated and then a bit alarmed. Had Victor suffered some kind of relapse or infection, had Lora driven him to the hospital?

He stepped back into the kitchen and switched on all the lights. He finally found a handwritten note attached to the refrigerator door with a magnet.

"Going stir crazy," Victor had written. "Lora suggests we tour the mall. Took Bow Wow with us. Don't wait up."

The mall?

What was a man who couldn't walk, except to hobble about on crutches, doing at a mall? Who else in the world would take a recovering man and a high-strung dog to a place like that?

He didn't even know Lora liked to shop. Trina lived to shop, but Lora?

Feeling vaguely disappointed and utterly confounded, he pulled out his cell phone and called Trina. She answered on the first ring, her well-modulated voice full of anticipation. Once she got over the disappointment that he wasn't a casting director calling back, she sounded happy to hear from him.

On Tuesday, Lora met Arthur Polanski at the dry cleaners. She was picking up her grandmother's good sweaters and Arthur worked behind the counter. He was a portly man with a slight flush to his face, pushing eighty, she thought. He said he worked part-time for his son who owned the store. He also said that he'd just moved to Fern Glen to be near his son's family and hinted that he was a little lonely.

There's a cure for that, Lora thought as she dug around in her purse for a Lora Dunes Florist business card.

She handed it to Arthur with a flourish. "Bring this card in on Friday afternoon and receive a free carnation," she told him. "It's a promotional gimmick, but you have nothing to lose. Just ask for Ella." To make sure he remembered, she'd previously scribbled her grandmother's name on the back of the card.

Arthur had a really nice smile and almost all his own teeth. He also had a full head of hair. He took a dollar off the dry cleaning bill which Lora thought was quite gallant.

The idea had come to Lora the night before as she pushed Dr. Reed's wheelchair through the crowded shopping mall. She'd just picked up a new batch of business cards from the printer when she saw the elderly man buying an ice-cream cone for himself and the thought occurred to her. *What a waste,* she'd thought. *He's alone, Gram's alone...how could I get them together?*

Why not plot a few little meetings of her own, she'd decided, and digging the box of cards out of the bag, started handing them out to likely candidates with the carnation as bait and Grandma as first prize. For a while, she considered straggling the days, mentioning Monday to one and Thursday to another, but that seemed doomed to failure as her grandmother was in and out of the shop so much lately. She'd settled on one free-for-all day and time: Friday afternoon.

The plan was ingenious in its simplicity. If the man was married or attached to someone else, he got a free carnation and the store got a little publicity for a nominal cost. If he was alone and if the pretty lady with the wispy white hair and bright blue eyes appealed to him and him to her— well, watch out world, wedding bells might ring twice. Once for Dr. Reed and her mother and once for Grandma and Lucky Bachelor Number Whatever!

But not for Lora.

She'd handed out about a dozen cards before leaving the mall. It was hard to know for sure because she'd ended up misplacing the bag with the box of cards in it. She thought it might be in Dr. Reed's trunk or somewhere in the cluttered dining room no one actually used for eating, but thankfully, she still had a few extra at the shop, so the plan could proceed.

Meanwhile, she scurried back to the shop with Gram's dry cleaning in her arms, her mind focused on an arrangement she needed to make. She would use the plump Protea that always reminded Lora of green and pink artichokes, delicate purple orchids, spikes of red ginger, slender pink anthuriums, dark curly willow bark for interest. The client planned to give his wife this arrangement along with two tickets to Tahiti for her fortieth birthday and insisted on exotic, tropical flowers. Lora's supplier had done his best. Lora was even playing around with the idea of including a cute little bottle of sunscreen with the flowers.

Okay, maybe not. Maybe seashells glued to wires...

She walked in the front door of the shop and straight into a tall, well-built stranger.

"We'd just about given up on you," Lora's mom said, scurrying forward, taking the dry cleaning from Lora's arms, patting at Lora's disheveled hair and tweaking the floppy collar of her blue coat.

"Lora, honey, this is Michael Goodwin, the lovely man who owns the barbershop across the street. He came in to buy some flowers for his aunt, didn't you, Michael?"

Michael smiled in a lopsided way that made his thirty-something face look friendly and sincere at the same time. He had beautiful red hair cut very nicely and she wondered if he did it himself or if he went to another barber. His hazel eyes were clear and attractive. If it wasn't for the fact that his coloring bore a marked resemblance to the late, not-so-great Calvin, Lora might actually be interested in knowing this man. Might, that is, if she was interested in men at all, which at this juncture she most decidedly was not.

As it was, all she wanted to do was escape this awkward situation and go play with the flowers.

"Your mother has been telling me all about you," Michael said.

"Has she?" Lora said. "Well, you can't believe a word this woman says. She's only been out of the home for a few weeks, you know. We try to keep her inside—"

Angela Gifford nudged Lora. "Now you stop teasing Michael," she said with a nervous little laugh. "Help him find some flowers for his mother."

"You mean his aunt," Lora said dryly.

"Yes, his aunt."

"Actually, I was thinking I might like to get some flowers for my girlfriend," Michael said. "Yellow ones."

Lora's mom emitted a little gasp.

"I'll handle this, Mom," Lora said, laughing out loud inside but acting appropriately dignified on the outside. A girlfriend! How had her mother missed ascertaining that particularly useful bit of information? Wait, why had her mother tried to set her up with the barber when she'd witnessed Jon's kiss in Dr. Reed's garden?

Hmm—

"Come on, Michael, we took delivery of some beautiful tulips this morning. I'll get you set up," she said, leading him to the flower cooler. Lora's mom dumped Gram's dry cleaning onto the counter and stomped into the back room.

"Your mom seems upset," Michael whispered.

"It's time for her medication," Lora said sweetly.

"I didn't know he had a girlfriend," Lora's mom protested after Michael left with a dozen tulips. "He didn't tell me, honest. Will you ever forgive me?"

Lora stuck a heart-shaped anthurium into the shallow

upswept gold leaf bowl and said, "How many times do I have to tell you I'm not interested—"

"In men who aren't ready to settle down. But Michael has his own shop—"

"And a girlfriend," Lora said, ashamed at the impatience she could hear in her voice. Her mother had absolutely no learning curve. None!

Where was Jon? She'd made an emergency call and he'd assured her he could dart over to the shop during his lunch hour, which was now, so where was he?

He hadn't come home the night before. She'd fixed hazelnut-encrusted petrale sole, three pieces, and he hadn't even called, and he'd been in his room when she and Dr. Reed got home. Later, after she closed her own bedroom door, she heard Jon's voice and assumed he was helping Dr. Reed with his evening ablutions but the question remained.

Was Jon avoiding her and did it have something to do with that impulsive kiss and if it did, did that mean she was back in charge of the situation? It was one thing if she was rattled by his gesture, quite another if it had rattled him.

When had life gotten so complicated?

Her mother patted her hand. "Don't you worry, sweetheart, there are plenty of men out there. Gram and I will find you someone. Frankly, I think your grandmother is right, that Jon Woods fellow is just too good-looking."

"Where is Gram?"

"She got a phone call from someone at her church so now she's running errands. Anyway, your father said you could never trust a good-looking man and Victor says Jon has a movie star girlfriend, so you can see that Gram is right, he must be a playboy."

HELP!

As if in answer, the bell over the door rang and Lora looked up in time to catch Jon duck inside, his hair glistening with raindrops. She'd been so preoccupied that she hadn't even noticed it had started to rain.

My, but the man did look good wet.

She pictured him in the shower, rivulets running down his bronzed face, asking her to wash his back. She saw herself standing there in the steamy room, gaze averted, of course, but being such an all around good sport that it never occurred to her not to fulfill his modest request.

Of course, that meant she'd have to strip off her clothes and step into the shower and lather up his back, her soapy hands spreading across his slippery muscles—

"Lora, do you want me to get rid of him?" her mother asked.

Lora swallowed a lump as big as a giant bar of soap and shook her head. "No, no. I don't know where you got the feeling I don't like Jon, Mom. He's a charming man. I know about his girlfriend, we're just…friends."

"If he only wants to be friends, then why did he kiss you?"

"It's…it's complicated," Lora said. "I'll go see what he wants."

She approached Jon pondering this newfound problem of her mother thinking he was a two-timing rat when all Jon knew was that she'd called him and told him to get over here in a hurry and sweep her off her feet in front of her mother. He reached for her.

An image of the shower scene that had played itself out in her imagination sprang into her mind, but she pushed it away in time to sidestep him.

He leaned close and whispered in her ear and if the feel of his warm breath taunting her earlobe made her heartbeat quicken, it was simply residual fantasy and nothing else. He said, "I don't have much time. I have three surgeries this afternoon—"

"Change of plans," she whispered back. "Mom thinks you're cheating on Trina."

She could hear the catch in his breath. He finally said, "How does she know about Trina?"

"Dr. Reed told her. You're back to being labeled a playboy."

"Oh, brother."

"That kiss the other day was a big mistake."

"I thought—"

"You thought if you kissed me in front of Victor he would stop having ideas about me and my scheme to snare him would fall apart. Right?"

"Something like that."

"Except that he doesn't have ideas about me and I have never wanted to snare him."

He gripped her upper arms and stared into her eyes. His were deep and dark and so warm. When he spoke this time, it was at normal volume. "Let's go out later and discuss this like two friends. Can we do that?"

The ring of sincerity in his voice touched her. She said, "Yes. Of course." Her voice sounded like it came from the next room.

He dropped his hands, nodded in her mother's direction and left.

Lora went back to her flowers.

"He's not very romantic," her mother sniffed.

That's what you think, Lora thought, her arms still tingling where he'd gripped her, the memory of his lips way too vivid for comfort, the soft urgency of his voice echoing in her head and her imagination more than able to mix it all together.

"It stopped raining hours ago, let's take a walk," Jon said that night as Lora settled Dr. Reed in his favorite chair with Bow Wow and one of the two larger dogs curled on the rug in front of him. The smaller of the yellow dogs stood in the doorway, a coiled leash in her mouth.

"Sunny heard Jon use the 'W' word," Dr. Reed said. "I guess you're taking her with you on your walk."

"Are you sure you're okay being alone for a while?"

"Absolutely. There's a shoot 'em up movie on. Just move the phone closer and hand me the remote. You and Jon take your time."

Jon, who had insisted on washing the dishes by himself, snapped the leash on Sunny and then handed the dog her own lead which she carried with her head high, walking between the two humans, apparently unaware that neither one of them had control of her. They walked along the sidewalk for a while, but Dr. Reed's house was semirural and it wasn't long before the sidewalk gave way to a beaten path along the side of the road, and not long after that, the path disappeared altogether. They climbed over a split-rail fence and Jon unsnapped the dog and told her to go play.

Sunny scampered off, her feathery tail waving with excitement.

"This is a pretty piece of property," Lora said as she admired the grassy slope leading to a stream and the lush vegetation rimming the northern perimeter. Pale pink wild rhododendrons peeked out of the foliage and the view to the south was of the distant ocean.

"It's mine," Jon said, leaning down to straighten something that had fallen. Lora saw that it was a For Sale sign.

"Kids knock it down every couple of days," he added.

"Why do you have a piece of land in Fern Glen?"

He propped the sign against the fence and perched on the top rail. "It was my dad's. Victor and his wife built their house up here the year before Dad moved to Fern Glen to be Victor's partner. When this piece of land became available, I gather Dad bought it with the intention of building himself a house. He never got around to it. When he died, it came to me."

"Dr. Reed said your father's heart gave out."

"He'd had trouble for years, but I was under the impression he was better. He relied on Victor. That's why I owe Victor such a huge debt of gratitude and that's how I came to be a property owner in Fern Glen."

Lora looked around her. "It's lovely," she said, settling down beside him.

He said, "You're right, it is pretty." After a pause, he added, "Quiet. Lonely. Remote."

"You mention those things as though they're drawbacks."

"Aren't they?"

"No, of course not."

He swiveled to face her. "Lora, tell me the truth. Doesn't all this peace and tranquillity ever get to you?"

"What do you mean?"

He spread his arms. "I mean that all I can hear right now is the sound of my own voice."

"And the dog splashing in the creek and a bird chirping and the distant sound of the ocean and the buzz of a few insects—"

"Exactly. Nothing."

"Nothing? You have an odd view of what constitutes nothing."

"I mean," he said, staring into her eyes, "don't you ever long to get lost in a crowd or jostled on a boardwalk or hear people having a party or yelling at each other or cars honking...life!"

"Absolutely not!" she replied, horrified.

He popped to his feet and began walking. "Well, I do," he said.

Standing, she brushed off the seat of her pants. She'd expected a conversation, but not this one. She said, "How lucky for you that you live in southern California, then."

"Damn right," he said, turning to face her.

His expression was hard to read. Had talking about his

father upset him? Had she? Was it Fern Glen, could he really hate it here that much?

"Jon, what's wrong?"

He shook his head and looked away.

Lora walked past him toward the wooded area of the creek. A clump of wildflowers drew her attention and she knelt to look at it more closely. The delicate purple flowers were some of her favorites. Too bad they didn't last when picked.

"What's that?" John said.

"This?" She plucked one perfect flower and stood. Handing it to him, she said, "Wild Iris."

He twirled the stem between his fingers and finally said, "I called Trina last night."

"So, that's where you were."

"No, I called her after I got back to the house and found you and Victor off on an adventure."

"After dinner, he announced he was going nuts, said the walls were closing in on him."

"So you took him to a shopping mall. Interesting choice."

His tone irritated the devil out of her. What was with this guy? He was suspicious and distrustful and annoying. Should she mention her errand at the printing shop or the fact that Victor wanted a new robe? Absolutely not. She shrugged playfully and said, "The mall is the perfect place to accidentally run across a few dozen engagement rings, you know. There are dozens of jewelry stores, cases of big glittery diamonds. There's even a bridal shop in case he doesn't take the hint and if you really need to gild the lily, so to say, there's a naughty little lingerie store just bursting with silk undies."

"You," he said, dropping the blossom, "are incorrigible."

"I'm not the one who takes every opportunity to make a surly remark."

"I do not make surly remarks."

"You are the most aggravating man I've ever met. I never know where I stand with you."

"This is ripe. I can't believe you have the audacity to call me aggravating. I have half a mind to—"

"What, kiss me again?"

"Yes," he said, and just like that, she flung herself at him as he flung himself at her. They thudded together in the middle and it should have been awkward and painful, but instead, Lora swore she heard music playing.

She melted into his arms like a chocolate chip on a hot cookie sheet. She met his eager mouth with a kiss as long and deep as his, relishing every sensation, the smell of him, the taste, the strength, the desire. When she felt his tongue touch hers, her knees almost gave out or maybe they did, maybe he was holding her upright, she couldn't tell.

She knew she had to stop this, but that would take will-power, a commodity she didn't seem to have right that second. He pulled her down on the tall grass and put his arms around her as their knees touched the ground, and still his mouth devoured her and she did nothing to end a kiss that had trapped her heart like a mosquito in amber.

How did they end up lying side by side on the damp grass and how did his hand find its way under her jacket onto her bare skin and since when did the earth pulse in time with her thundering heartbeat and her insides threaten to explode?

He rolled on top of her, pinning her to the grass with his body. His hands beside her face, cushioned by her hair, he looked down into her eyes with the most tender expression she'd ever seen, then he lowered his head and kissed her again, and this time the kiss was almost gentle.

She could get lost, she realized as the warmth of his mouth reduced her to jelly. Lost forever...

She turned her face, and as he showered her neck with moist sensuous kisses she whispered one word.

"No."

Their eyes met and she saw comprehension flash through his irises.

"Jon, think of Trina."

He rolled off of her and lay beside her, his breath coming in ragged gasps and she mentally awarded herself a great big blue ribbon for using "admirable self-control under pressure," because, damn it, it didn't look as though anyone else was going to march across the grass and present her with a medal and she deserved accolades for being such an upstanding woman.

A credit, really, to all womankind.

Finally, he said, "I called her last night."

"Who?"

"Trina," he said, his voice so sexy she was beginning to reconsider. The world could keep its old blue ribbon—she'd take Jon.

No. No, no, no.

"You told me," she said.

"She can't come for a visit. Won't come."

And suddenly, everything was clear. Painfully clear. Horribly clear.

Trina wouldn't come, he was hurt. He might not be aware of his motives but Lora was: he was using her to assuage his hurt feelings and perhaps even to get back at Trina.

She said, "That's too bad," as she sat up and hugged her knees to her chest.

He sat up beside her. Pulling her hair aside, he kissed the back of her neck and she felt the touch of his lips shoot through her body and it took all the restraint she had not to lean back against him.

"I don't want to leave Victor alone for too long," she said.

He let her hair drop back into place. "You're beautiful, but so much more—"

"Stop," she said, twisting to face him. "Jon, this is all wrong."

He touched her cheek, sending shivers hither and yon. "It doesn't feel wrong."

"But it is."

"I don't think Trina cares." His finger traveled down her neck, played with the collar of her shirt. She yearned for his hand to keep right on traveling down her body, hitting the high spots, so to say, lighting little fires, big fires, holocausts, whatever. He added, "I don't know if she ever did care."

He was as bad as her mother, talking about one lover while attempting to woo another!

"This is wrong for me," she said firmly, gripping his hand and pushing it away from her. "Calvin left to go make his fortune in Chicago and I'm still here and I don't want to go through that again with another man. You're upset with Trina, but she's part of your normal life and pretty soon, you'll go home and things will go back to the way they were. And I'll still be here."

"You're not after Victor Reed," he said with no hint of a question in his voice.

She said, "No."

"Then why—"

"I wanted to get to know him. I thought that he and my mother might hit it off but I wasn't sure what kind of man he really was. And then he mentioned knowing my father. That made me feel kind of sad, I guess, because my dad left slowly and suddenly if you know what I mean."

"I wouldn't presume to know what you mean," Jon said.

"He'd been drifting away from Mom and me and the store for a long time but when he finally decided to actually leave, boom, he was out of here. Now I only talk to him on the phone every month or so. He sounds happy, which should make me happy for him, but somehow doesn't. Anyway, when I spoke to him Sunday night, he mentioned a new girlfriend and that he might not be available to talk to me for a while. I got mad at him. He told me I don't understand. He's right.''

''You miss your father,'' Jon said.

''No—''

''Yes you do. I miss mine, too.''

Lora thought about this a moment. Jon was right, she did miss her father. Why did he have to leave, why was he now pushing her away? Did all men do this to the women who loved them, be they wives, daughters... fiancées? In a moment of blinding honesty, she said, ''I think when the opportunity to spend some time with Dr. Reed presented itself, I grabbed it. I liked him right away, you know. He was so...well, kind.''

''Like a father.''

''No.''

Jon looked down and then up again. ''So, you're matchmaking for your mother. Does she know?''

''No.''

''And she's matchmaking for you.''

''She's trying. All I ever wanted from you was a decoy romance so Mom and Gram would get off my back while I find the two of them distractions of their own so I can work in the greenhouse in peace.''

''Plus you wanted to mislead me.''

''That, too.''

''So, what is it you do in that mysterious greenhouse?''

''It's simple. I'm trying to secure our future,'' she said. ''And you haven't stopped loving Trina, Jon. Not so quickly, not just because she can't fly up here for a visit.''

Standing, he offered her a hand and pulled her to her feet just as Sunny, dripping wet from her romp in the creek, shook and wiggled about their legs.

''Nothing smells quite like a wet dog,'' Jon said, and they both laughed though there was nothing funny about being soaked by a goofy dog while trying to disavow what they had just shared.

Lora started walking, her emotions tumbling against one another like jawbreakers in a kid's pocket. She felt a renewed sense of loss, both for her father and for Calvin. She felt confused about Jon, jealous of Trina, uneasy about something she couldn't even define.

When they were almost back at the house, he caught her arm. "Lora?"

She turned and waited.

"I liked kissing you," he said. "If I loved Trina, would I like kissing you?"

"I don't know," she said without admitting that she'd liked kissing him, too, more than liked it if truth be known, and yet it seemed to be tearing her up inside as well.

She said, "I think we're both at some sort of crossroads, Jon. There's a lot going on. That kiss wasn't real, it was a byproduct of everything else."

He looked unconvinced, but at this point, she felt she knew his motives better than he did. It wasn't that he didn't love Trina, it was that she'd hurt him, and damn but she was not going to be five foot one inches of comfort food for a lonely out-of-town veterinarian!

He finally said, "Let your mother and grandmother think I've broken off with Trina and that you and I are now dating," he added. "Victor doesn't like Trina—not that he's ever met her—so he won't care and a month from now, I'll be gone and none of this will matter. Nothing has changed."

But to Lora, it seemed everything had changed. She said, "I'll think about it. You and Victor are getting along so well, maybe I should pack my bag and go home. There's work to be done in the greenhouse and I...well, I'll bet you anything my fish miss me something awful."

Looking down at her, he said, "I read somewhere that a goldfish has a memory span of three seconds. That means that by the time it reaches one end of the bowl, the other end is a mystery.''

"Then why do the fish get all excited in the morning when I turn their lights on and feed them?''

"Hmm—maybe a conditioned response.''

"Or maybe they remember that the light means food.''

"Or maybe they just like looking up through the water and seeing you looking down at them.''

They stared at each other.

"Don't go," he said at last. "If you're uncomfortable having me around, I'll leave.''

"Dr. Reed needs you," she said, thinking of how the older man relied on the younger man's strength and gentleness to help him at night and how awkward it would be for him if Lora tried to take over. She wasn't thinking of what it would be like to be in that house without Jon.

"He needs you, too," Jon said. "I may help him physically, but your cooking and laughter...well, you help his heart.''

That was about the nicest thing anyone had ever said to her. She met his gaze and felt a sigh building in her stomach, of all places. Maybe she was hungry. There was a half gallon of fudge ripple ice cream in the freezer. Wait, she ate dinner only an hour ago. Was she hungry or depressed? Eating for hunger was okay, eating from depression could mean a trip to the store for bigger clothes.

"Besides, what about your mother?" he continued. "What about the barber across the street?''

Lora knew the barber was out of the running, but what about the next hapless male to come under her mother's or grandmother's scrutiny? One thing for certain: she was going to grab that ice cream and a spoon as soon as she hit the house.

She said, "Okay, okay, you made your point. I'm warning you, though. For this to work, you're going to have to figure out a way to get back in Mom's and Gram's favor. Good luck.''

''I'll need it,'' he said, peering over her head. ''Look. Isn't that—''

Lora turned slowly and found a small green car parked in Dr. Reed's driveway. ''My mother's car?'' she finished for him. ''It sure is.''

She was suddenly aware of the damp condition of both of their backsides, of the squished purple iris blossom now plastered to Jon's sleeve.

As Jon plucked the leaves from her hair and she peeled away the iris, another thought struck her: she recalled the way Dr. Reed had insisted she move the phone close to his chair before she left.

Had he called her mother?

Was romance blooming?

Please, please, please, just let it be two-sided!

Chapter Six

"Just hold my hand and try not to argue with me or look like you want to knock my lights out," Jon told Lora as he opened the front door.

"What are you going to do?" she whispered.

"I don't know, I'll think of something. Just follow my lead."

"But—"

"There you go," he said, exasperated. "You just can't help yourself, can you?"

At that moment, apparently frustrated with all the time they were taking to get through the door, Sunny burst between them, knocked the door wide open and ran headlong into Hobo, the other big dog who had apparently been lurking inside. The two of them twisted and turned, knocking Jon aside and Lora to the tile floor, then they took off down the hall at a good clip, snarling and playing as they went.

Jon picked Lora up and set her straight. "Are you okay?"

From the den, they could hear Victor's frantic commands. "Get down! Stop shaking!" They also heard barking, Victor's hurried apologies and a couple of female squeals.

"I'm fine," Lora said, limping down the hall. "Hurry, save Victor and my mom."

By the time he got to the den, Sunny had seemingly been everywhere. There were muddy footprints on the rug, drops of water on the television screen, scattered newspapers and an overturned silk plant. Lora's mom stood hugging herself in one corner, her pale yellow skirt now streaked with brown, Victor had a hand on Sunny's leash and Lora's grandmother had retreated to the big leather chair by the window along with the cats. Bow Wow stood in the middle of the crowded room, yipping in excitement while Hobo chimed in with a deep "woof," every once in a while.

Jon dragged Sunny and Hobo into the backyard and returned to the den. Lora's mother was dabbing at her skirt with what looked like a handkerchief—no doubt, one of Victor's—Lora was straightening Victor's lap blanket and Bow Wow had settled down on his bed.

"No need to fuss," Victor said, shooing Lora away.

"I'm sorry about Sunny—"

Victor patted her hand and gave her such a paternal look that Jon wondered how he'd ever thought there was anything sexual between them. Victor said, "Now, honey. Sunny is a big galoot, I know that about her, and Hobo isn't much better. Both of them have hearts of gold, but they're also challenged in the brain department. Angela, I'll pay the dry cleaning bill for your skirt. Elloise, how are you doing over there with all those cats?"

Jon's gaze swiveled to Lora's grandmother. All three of the cats were perched on or about the plump little woman, the black cat perched on the very top of the chair, the gray and white on the arm and the white one on Elloise's lap. She was stroking Frosty and smiling.

"What a commotion! It's a zoo here, Vic, a regular zoo. But this little cat, well, he's a pip."

Jon noticed Lora still limping as she tried to pick up the plant. He did it for her, then took her arm and half supported her, ignoring the frown that creased her brow as she glanced at him and also ignoring the warmth and softness of her body clenched to his side.

He helped her sit then kneeled in front of her. "Give me your foot," he said softly.

After a slight hesitation, she raised her leg and settled her foot in his hands. He took off her shoe and pared away her sock.

What nice feet, but whoa! She'd painted her toenails a shocking electric green. As he gaped, she wiggled her toes and when he met her gaze, she grinned through a wince. He held her heel, trying hard not to notice her fine bone structure or the glimpse of her calf as it disappeared up her pant leg. He concentrated on gently palpitating her ankle.

"I'm not one of your puppy-dogs or kitty-cats," Lora said.

"Anatomy is anatomy, broken bones is broken bones," he told her. He added, "But thankfully, your ankle is just twisted. I'll get you an ice pack."

"Are you sure nothing else is wrong with her?" Lora's mom said, advancing.

"I'm sure," Jon said as he stood.

"That's good because she has a date later tonight. Lora, you'll be so excited to know that the barber has a younger, unattached brother! He sells shoes. He loves Fern Glen. I've set everything up."

Lora's expression went from amused to desperate and for a second, Jon toyed around with the idea of leaving her hanging out there to blow in the wind all by herself. Serve her right for the puppy-dog/kitty-cat crack. However, he was a kind-hearted man who had promised to help this odd little damsel in distress.

"She's okay, but not up to going out," he said firmly.

"She and Ronald can watch television."

"She needs complete rest," he said.

"What's more relaxing than gazing at a television screen with a thoughtful young man in attendance?"

"Going straight to bed with two aspirin."

Mrs. Gifford shook her head. "It's up to Lora," she said.

This woman was formidable! No wonder Lora was frantic. He countered with a pleasant, "Of course."

Lora said, "I think Jon is right, Mom. I think I'd be more comfortable staying right here tonight. In my bedroom, I mean. Alone."

Angela Gifford smiled. "How about I call Ronald and tell him tomorrow night?"

A deep tsking sound was followed by a snappy, "Oh, for heaven's sake, Angela, can't you see that these two are involved with one another?"

This comment came from Lora's grandmother and was followed with a perky, "Am I right, kids?"

Lora bit her lip and nodded.

Jon said, "That's right." He leaned down and brushed his lips against Lora's, and then before he knew what he was doing, he kissed her again.

Petals, grass, summer days, that's what Lora Gifford's lips reminded him of. He found that his hand had strayed to her hair and that a few glossy strands had snuck their way between his fingers. Her eyes were deep with emotion or worry or embarrassment.

What in the world was he doing?

Getting into his part, that's what. This had nothing to do with the encounter in the field when they'd thrown themselves into each other's arms and kissed with wild abandon, as though they had a right to kiss like that, as though it made even a speck of good sense.

Or did it?

Maybe he should enroll in acting school when he got home; perhaps he was a natural-born method actor totally immersed in the role of Lora's potential lover without his conscious mind having a clue about what was going on! He was talented, that was all.

He was in trouble. He needed Trina and his own life, he needed reality. This room, no this whole bucolic town, was a stage, Lora the beguiling heroine, his actions part of a spontaneous, ongoing script over which he had no control.

Maybe he would fly home next weekend and see Trina. Excellent idea!

He straightened and faced the three older people in the room. "I'll get that ice pack," he mumbled like the confused idiot he was.

Lora's mom sighed.

Lora's grandmother said, "I'll take an ice pack, too, if you stick it in a glass and splash some vodka over it."

"Forget the ice pack, just bring the fudge ripple ice cream," Lora called. "And a spoon."

Victor chuckled.

Lora lay awake that night. Her ankle still hurt, though not badly. What kept her from sleep was the worry that she was getting too attached to Jon.

She knew where his feelings came from, but what about her own?

He would leave soon and judging from the disparaging things he said about Fern Glen, he wouldn't look back, not ever.

She had just realized tonight that she was still on the rebound from Calvin, that his walking away two months after they'd set a wedding date had hurt her more deeply than she'd ever let on even to herself, and that her mother and grandmother constantly forcing men and relationships on her was making her more than nuts. It was making her…well, super nuts.

And Jon wasn't helping.

This charade they were in, these kisses, the way he looked at her and the way her heart ached for him, well, none of this was helping.

And yet it seemed to be working. Her mother had called and canceled the date with Ronald, her grandmother looked at her with a smile in her eyes as though thinking, "Ah, young love!" If this meant they would leave her alone, wasn't it worth the price?

Worth a broken heart?

She had to do something.

Without turning on the light, she more or less hopped to the window and peered into the backyard, at the dark shapes of the bushes and the glowing white form of the gazebo and it wasn't until a shadow shifted that she realized Jon was out there, sitting in the gazebo.

Thinking about Trina…

Thinking about leaving…

If he thought about her at all, it was through a haze of confusion. She was available and part of a charade that had turned out to be tricky in the emotion department. Trina had hurt him when she refused to come for a visit.

All Lora wanted, what she knew she needed to keep in focus, was her project in the greenhouse, the eventual financial gain to be made, the ultimate revamping of the florist shop and the accompanying success.

She looked at Jon's shape again, and then as she turned, she saw the bedside phone and made a decision. Tomorrow, she would start making this problem go away so she could concentrate on her project, and, of course, her mom and Dr. Reed's romance.

It seemed to Lora as though it was stalled. Take tonight's visit, for example: her mom had said she'd come over to bring Dr. Reed a book on vegetable gardening. Then why had she brought along Gram? Didn't she understand that three was a crowd?

Gram had giggled her way through the evening, kissing the cats and letting Bow Wow sit on her lap while her mother stared endlessly at a framed photograph of a fish that hung on Dr. Reed's wall.

Geez.

Well, Friday ought to take care of that when a dozen or so seventy-plus-year-old gentlemen showed up toting business cards marked *Ella,* asking for carnations. Gram would have so many new romantic interests her tagging along days would come to an end.

Lora limped back to bed.

She held her hand up in the dark and ticked off indistinct fingers.

Call the lawyers and see if any progress had been made on her patent.

Order carnations.

Stay away from Jon.

Call Trina.

Jon pushed open the door and found himself standing amidst hundreds if not thousands of bottles of wine. He glanced at a few of the labels, recognized a handful, even thought of buying one for dinner, then the thought fled. Approaching from behind the counter along the north wall was a very attractive woman in form-fitting red slacks and a white blouse. There wasn't so much as a flicker of recognition in her almond-shaped eyes.

"May I help you?" she asked.

"Yes, as a matter of fact you can. I'm here about your cat—"

Her pretty eyes narrowed as recognition flooded her face. "I know you. You're that veterinarian!"

Play the **Lucky Hearts** Game

and get...

2 FREE BOOKS
and a **FREE MYSTERY GIFT...**
YOURS to KEEP!

yes! I have scratched off the silver card. Please send me my *2 FREE BOOKS* and *FREE mystery GIFT*. I understand that I am under no obligation to purchase any books as explained on the back of this card.

Scratch Here!

then look below to see what your cards get you... 2 Free Books & a Free Mystery Gift!

309 SDL DZ5R   209 SDL DZ56

FIRST NAME

LAST NAME

ADDRESS

APT.#

CITY

STATE/PROV.

ZIP/POSTAL CODE

(S-R-06/04)

Twenty-one gets you
2 FREE BOOKS
and a *FREE MYSTERY GIFT!*

Twenty gets you
2 FREE BOOKS!

Nineteen gets you
1 FREE BOOK!

TRY AGAIN!

Offer limited to one per household and not valid to current Silhouette Romance® subscribers. All orders subject to approval.

The Silhouette Reader Service™ — Here's how it works:

Accepting your 2 free books and mystery gift places you under no obligation to buy anything. You may keep the books and gift and return the shipping statement marked "cancel." If you do not cancel, about a month later we'll send you 6 additional books and bill you just $3.34 each in the U.S., or $3.80 each in Canada, plus 25¢ shipping & handling per book and applicable taxes if any.* That's the complete price and — compared to cover prices of $3.99 each in the U.S. and $4.50 each in Canada — it's quite a bargain! You may cancel at any time, but if you choose to continue, every month we'll send you 6 more books, which you may either purchase at the discount price or return to us and cancel your subscription.

*Terms and prices subject to change without notice. Sales tax applicable in N.Y. Canadian residents will be charged applicable provincial taxes and GST. Credit or debit balances in a customer's account(s) may be offset by any other outstanding balance owed by or to the customer.

If offer card is missing write to: The Silhouette Reader Service, 3010 Walden Ave., P.O. Box 1867, Buffalo, NY 14240-1867

BUSINESS REPLY MAIL

FIRST-CLASS MAIL   PERMIT NO. 717-003   BUFFALO, NY

POSTAGE WILL BE PAID BY ADDRESSEE

SILHOUETTE READER SERVICE
3010 WALDEN AVE
PO BOX 1867
BUFFALO NY 14240-9952

NO POSTAGE
NECESSARY
IF MAILED
IN THE
UNITED STATES

"Now, Mrs. Pullman—"

"I told you, I don't want the cat."

"Yes," he said calmly, "I recall you saying that. But you can't just abandon her at our office. It doesn't work that way."

"Someone abandoned her in our alley," she said. "Same thing."

"Mrs. Pullman, perhaps if I talk to your husband about this. You said he was fond of the little animal. Maybe he and I can find—"

"He was going to be home Friday but he called last night and said he's extending his trip another few days," she said. "And I didn't say he was fond of her, I said he fed her. It's not the same thing. You're the animal lover, you keep the cat."

"I can't. You have an office bill to settle—"

"I'll pay my bill," she snapped. She thought for a second and added, "You say the cat is mine?"

"That's right."

"Then put her to sleep! I'll pay for it. End of case. Now, if you'd like to browse or if you'd like me to recommend a vintage—"

"Put her to sleep!" Jon yelled, startling an older couple near the back of the store. "There's nothing wrong with her. The kittens are almost full-term. What kind of heartless—"

"Please lower your voice," she said with a nervous glance at her customers.

Jon forced his clenched hands to relax. He forced himself to lower his voice. He said, "Mrs. Pullman, please pay Dr. Reed's office what you owe and forget about the cat, go back to making money." He turned on his heels and tried to slam the door behind him, but it was one of the pressure controlled kind and wouldn't slam. He kicked it instead, then took off down the sidewalk at a brisk pace, the pedestrians and traffic all around him a blur.

People!

He strode right past his car and yanked open the florist shop door. The place was empty, and once again, he was struck with how outdated it looked.

Lora peeked from the back and smiled when she saw him. Her smile helped calm him down a little. He saw no sign of her family and was glad.

"Come on back," she called.

He went through the partition separating retail space from work space and was immediately immersed in a bounty of flowers. Every color, every shape and size. The beauty was stunning, the aroma soothing.

Lora was elbow deep in petals and greenery. "I just took delivery," she informed him. "I'm in the process of prepping everything for the cooler." She cocked her head and looked at him closely and he tried to relax, tried not to look as angry as he felt.

"Grab a stool," she said. "There are some clippers over there. Why don't you help me? Take half an inch or so off the end of the stems."

He found the stool and the clippers as Lora plopped a tall urn of flowers he didn't recognize down in front of him. He watched her do a couple and then he started. She didn't speak and he was still too frustrated to say anything, but gradually he found the work calmed his nerves a little and after a silent but productive fifteen minutes, he started to come out of his funk.

He tried his voice. "How's your ankle?"

"Much better. Barely a limp."

"Where are your matchmakers?"

"They're delivering flowers." As she spoke, her hands moved automatically, removing thorns and leaves, shedding outer layers of petals on a rose until she was left with a succulent bud, threading a wire up through the base, wrapping it with green tape, snipping the end and storing it in a vat of cool water. He wondered how many times she'd done this.

"What happened to you?" she asked.

He shook his head.

"Come on, Jon, you came in here looking like you'd like to pummel someone."

"Heartless people," he said softly. "I hate heartless, selfish people. That's all."

With her good foot, she nudged another fragrant urn his way, this one full of red and white carnations. "Same drill," she said. "Tell me about your own practice down in Beverly Hills."

He started snipping as he spoke. "Well, it's a great place to work. A brand-new building, state-of-the-art equipment, wonderful people to work with. The partners are a husband and wife team, though they've offered to let me buy in when I get back, which I'll do. Ellen is great with cats, Bob has a thing for exotic pets and my specialty is house calls, especially to the elderly or infirm. There are several white-haired ladies who think of me as a second son. I can't tell you how many tea sandwiches I've eaten."

"You love working there."

"Yes," he said, feeling better with every cut stem, more grounded with every memory Lora coaxed from his brain. "Ellen and Bob are great people. My being away is a strain on them."

"You can't wait to get back. You're homesick."

He stared at her and smiled. "Is it that obvious?"

She shrugged.

"There are a lot of things I miss," he said.

"I know I would miss the people here if I ever left," Lora said. "Mom and Gram are presently rather annoying, but usually they're great. I think Mom is worried you'll break my heart. I'll have to make sure she thinks that I'm the one who terminates our fledging love affair when you go home."

"We'll stage a big fight," Jon said. "You can tell me I'm not good enough for you and to get lost."

"And the fact that I never really loved you will mean I'll bounce back so fast her head will spin! I must have moped something terrible after Calvin left to have her overreact this way now. Hopefully by then she'll be engaged to Dr. Reed and my love life will have all the relevance of a poinsettia the day after Christmas."

"Yeah," he said, and concentrated on his chore.

The door behind them opened and Gram breezed in, her fine white hair fluttering around her cheerful face. She looked at the two of them and smiled. "Deliveries made. Anything exciting happen while I was gone?"

"Not a thing," Lora said. "Where's Mom?"

"Off on some secret errand," Gram said with a wink.

"With Dr. Reed?" Lora asked, her voice hopeful.

Lora's grandmother shrugged. "She wouldn't say. I'm going to go dust the silk flowers."

Jon got to his feet. "And I'd better get back to Victor's office."

Lora did a little number with her eyes that seemed to be reminding him that it was just as important for Jon to make her grandmother believe in their attraction as it was her mother. He leaned over Lora and kissed the top of her perfumed head. Her hair was soft and much less dangerous than her lips. "I'll see you tonight," he said.

She smiled and he took off.

He skipped dinner that night though he did leave a message with Victor advising him of this so Lora wouldn't cook too much food again. He went to the beach, hoping to run into Nolan and his dog, Bill, but there wasn't a glimpse of them or of the old black truck. After his solitary run, he took a chance and drove to Nolan's house.

The idea he was about to implement had come to him during his late night think-a-thon in the gazebo when he realized he was losing his sense of self-identity and Lora was largely to blame. That wasn't fair, of course, it was a lot more complicated than that, but something had to be done and this was all he could think of. He got out of the car and took a deep breath of cool, salty air.

The door opened as he approached and Bill woofed a greeting.

Jon ruffled the dog's ears. "Sorry to drop by like this," he called, "but you don't have a phone and I wanted to see how Bill was doing. And talk to you."

Nolan was dressed in the same near rags as before, his hair caught in a low ponytail, his eyes downcast. He had smears of blue and green paint on his hands as though he'd been working. He said, "No problem. How about a home brew?"

"You're busy," Jon said, gesturing at Nolan's hands. "I don't want to be in the way."

"Just finished a seascape," Nolan said. "I never tried a seascape before but a lady wanted one. I don't know if it's any good. Maybe you could tell me."

Jon laughed. "I could give you an uneducated opinion," he said.

The two men went into the house, the centerpiece of which was a circular wood-burning fireplace crackling with flame. The room felt overly warm to Jon after the cool breeze outside. Nolan worked at a table topped with a piece of plywood propped up by a couple of books on each side to give it a slight tilt. Taped to the plywood was a sheet of paper and covering the sheet was a splendid painting of dunes and waves as seen from the top of the nearby bluff.

"It's good," Jon said as Nolan handed him a beer.

Nolan stood back and studied it for a moment. Then as he picked up his brushes and palette, he called, "Thanks," over his shoulder.

"It's hard to believe it's your first effort."

Nolan ran water over everything in the sink and returned, drying his hands on a rag. "It was kind of fun. Maybe I'll try something else different."

"If you ever do another seascape, I'll buy it from you." Jon was thinking that a watercolor of the vast, uninhabited beach would look great framed and hanging in his office back home, and would also serve as a reminder of this place and this time.

Nolan nodded. "Sure."

The two men took their beer to Nolan's sagging sofa. The dog had claimed the middle, so Jon sat on one end and Nolan on the other. Jon had something he wanted to say to Nolan and he wasn't quite sure how to start. He casually examined the dog's perfectly healed foot as they talked about the weather for a while until Nolan opened up about painting wildflowers, showing palatable vitality as he discussed the merits of this artist over that one. When things grew quiet again, Jon sucked in his breath and forged ahead. "Nolan, I know it's none of my business, but do you have a girlfriend?"

Nolan's fair skin actually mottled with red as he said, "Talking to women is...difficult."

"Boy, isn't that the truth," Jon said. The two men shook their heads and took a swallow of beer.

"Thing is," Jon added at last, "I know a woman. She's smart, she's pretty, she's nice. I was wondering if you might like to take her out."

Nolan spared him a quick glance. "What's wrong with her?"

"Nothing," Jon said, her slender ankle and bright green toenails flashing across his mind. If pressed he would have to admit that she was a trifle argumentative and more than a little quirky. Silly, sometimes. Stuck in this piece of the earth like a redwood tree. Distrustful of men...

"Not a damn thing," he growled. "She's great. She

works with flowers. She loves Fern Glen. It seems you and she might have a lot in common.''

Nolan narrowed his eyes which gave him a shrewd look so at odds with his usual appearance. ''Then why don't you take her out?''

''I already have a girlfriend,'' he said.

''Oh.''

''And I like you and I like Lora so it occurred to me that the two of you might like each other.'' This sounded so high school that Jon wished he could think of a way to extricate himself from the whole conversation. How could words that sounded so reasonable when rehearsed alone in a car sound so pathetic when spoken aloud?

Nolan gazed at his shoes, then at Jon and said, ''I'm not really very interesting to most women. Women like men who dress better and talk like you.''

Forging ahead, Jon said, ''Listen, we're about the same size. I have lots of clothes. You're welcome to some. I'll help you learn a few conversational gambits. I just want you to meet Lora. You'll, well, you'll like her. Everyone likes her. How could you not like her?''

Nolan looked Jon in the eye and again exhibited unexpected perception by asking, ''Why is it so important to you?''

Jon opened his mouth and closed it with a sigh. The truth was too personal, too complicated, too shrouded in mystery like the age-old myth of the ancient pyramids. He compromised and said, ''I think she's lonely. I can't date her so I thought you might like the opportunity to meet her.'' Suddenly cooling on the whole absurd idea, he added, ''Listen, let's forget the whole thing, I'll never mention it again.''

''Let me think about it,'' Nolan said.

Jon nodded. He'd thought he'd feel better at this point. He thought that trying to match Lora up with Nolan would get her out of his head where she didn't belong. He

planned to call Trina tonight and inform her of his decision
to fly home for the weekend. Maybe Lora and Nolan could
go out to dinner or maybe Lora would come here, maybe
she'd make Nolan dinner in his cramped cluttered kitchen
and later they could sit on the sofa together, watching the
fire burn, no need for words.

A man, a woman, a blazing fire.

Wine.

Her luscious lips. The aqua dress. Her hair an ebony
cloud of silk. Her legs. Her green toenails...

The dog between them. Yeah. He liked that picture better. Bill probably always sat in the middle of the sofa;
Nolan and Lora would have to look at each other over the
dog's shaggy body. He patted Bill's flank.

Never mind, the point was that his part in this was of-
ficially over. Nolan would or wouldn't take out Lora, Lora
would or wouldn't like Nolan, the wheels were in motion,
he could sit by and pat himself on the back if things
worked out and discreetly disappear if they didn't. Everyone else in town seemed to be matchmaking, why not him?

He patted Bill's flank again and declined another beer.

He just hoped Lora never got wind that he'd set her up.

Nolan said, "I thought about it. The answer is yes. I
don't need to borrow clothes. My father got married again
ten years ago and he gave me this really cool blue tuxedo.
I've never had a chance to wear it."

Jon said, "I can't think of a place in Fern Glen that
requires something quite so...sophisticated, Nolan."

"Too fancy, huh?"

"Maybe."

"Yeah, I guess you're right."

"Let's aim for Saturday night," Jon told Nolan and
made a mental note to bring a stack of clothes over before
then.

All that was left to do was figure out a way to get Lora
to consent to all this.

Chapter Seven

Lora's heart pounded like a kid trying to hammer a peg in a hole as the phone on the other end of the line rang and rang. No way was she going to leave a message, so she was about to hang up when she heard a sparkling, "Hiya. This is Trina!"

Lora had written a little script for herself. She looked at the paper now and tried to read the words, but they had magically transformed themselves from English to scribbles resembling Mandarin Chinese and didn't make sense no matter how many times she turned the paper.

"Hello?" Trina chirped, her voice now tinged with suspicion. "Is anyone there?"

Lora raised her voice an octave and whispered, "Yes, yes." She didn't want Dr. Reed to hear her talking and she was terrified Jon would come home and walk into the kitchen and find her on the phone, standing between the wall and the refrigerator, a broom and a dust mop for company, plotting behind his back. She added, "Sorry."

"Are you anyone?" Trina said briskly.

"I beg your pardon?"

"In the movies? Wait, is this a telemarketer because if it is, you can just take my number off your list and—"

"I'm not a telemarketer," Lora said. Taking a deep breath, she added, "I'm a…friend…of Jon Woods."

"Oh. Well, Jon isn't in town right now. What did you say your name is?"

"I didn't. I know he's not down there because he's up here with me, if you get my drift."

"What drift? Who is this?"

"A friend of Jon's," Lora said and tried to titter. It sounded more like she was strangling on cookies.

"What do you want?" Trina said.

"I just want to know where you stand."

"Stand on what?"

"On Jon. On your relationship. After all, I have scruples."

Trina said, "Good for you."

"I don't want to steal a man from another woman."

Trina's voice had already lost its cheery note, but now it got downright icy as she said, "Let me get this straight. You're trying to move in on *my* boyfriend?"

"He's just so sexy," Lora said, figuring no woman liked to hear the supposed competition call her man sexy. But he *was* sexy, overtly so, and for just an instant, she was flat on her back, the damp grass beneath her, Jon's warm heavy weight on top of her, his eyes delving into hers and her body on fire. She got so dizzy she damn near fainted.

She reached out to steady herself and was attacked by the broom.

Trina snapped, "Like I need *you* to tell *me* that? I'm warning you, back off."

Lora rubbed her head and sandwiched the phone between chin and shoulder. "Well, if you care about him—" she began as she wrestled the broom back into place.

"Why don't you just wait until I tell Jon I'm coming

up there this weekend and see how fast he tells you to get lost!''

Aha! ''Don't mention this call—''

''Now, why would I mention this call? Get over yourself!'' With that the phone line went dead and Lora, breathing a heavy sigh of relief and sporting a sore spot on her forehead, clicked off the phone.

Job done. Mission accomplished.

Complication: Would her mother get wind of Trina's visit and if she did, would it imply to her that Lora and Jon had broken up and Lora was once again available for matchmaking? In other words, was Lora sabotaging her own devious plans by arranging this little visit?

Solution: Fancy footwork, discreet misdirection, luck.

Question: Was Trina motivated by possessiveness or love?

Answer: Did it matter as long as the woman got on a plane and came to see Jon and reminded him who he was and who he loved? But honestly, could someone like Jon really love someone like Trina? The woman sounded like a scheming hussy.

Okay, okay, not the point.

Trina was coming, lured by another woman's feigned interest.

That was the point.

Some people were just so predictable.

Jon hung up the phone and felt a combination of excitement and disbelief tinged with a little uneasiness. Trina had booked a flight north.

She was coming for ten days.

Ten days!

Good thing Victor had just about outgrown any need for someone to help him at night. If there was one thing Jon couldn't visualize it was Trina and Lora and him all living in Victor's house. Throw in the occasional visit by Lora's mom and it was a recipe made in hell.

Trina would arrive Saturday afternoon. It was time to move back to the apartment.

Another thought followed that one so closely that Jon grinned.

He'd be in Fern Glen over the weekend! He could go along on Nolan and Lora's date. He could help Nolan over the rough spots, he could keep the conversation flowing, he could make sure the date didn't end up on Nolan's sofa.

Trina could go, too, of course.

This was a great idea. He'd bring Nolan up to speed when he took over a few items of clothing. Then he'd talk to Lora and explain about Trina's surprise visit. He'd tell her Trina wanted to meet her. Would Lora fall for it?

Ha! Lora was as curious as a cat. Of course she'd want to meet Trina and he could explain Nolan's presence by explaining that Nolan was a talented painter who was anxious to meet a beautiful, interesting woman, i.e. Lora. Flattered, she would be ripe for the picking.

Ripe for romance.

Whatever. What she was or wasn't ripe for was none of his business.

This was a noble thing he was doing, matching Lora and Nolan. More noble for Nolan, perhaps, seeing as the man didn't look like he'd had a date since he started sprouting facial hair. Speaking of facial hair, a trip to a good barber was definitely in order.

Now Lora, on the other hand, was infinitely datable. He doubted she needed his or anyone else's help in that department, but getting her to let go of her past, well, that was different.

She had for a moment though, he'd felt it in her kiss, he'd seen it in her eyes. For a moment, she'd been his.

Why?

Not one to kid himself about his charms, he had to wonder.

The answer was obvious. He was safe. He was with Trina and Lora knew it, in fact, she'd brought Trina's name up at a most telling moment. She probably felt guilty for indulging herself at his expense!

Nolan was the one he should be worrying about, not Lora!

Never mind.

By Sunday morning, it would all be over and he could concentrate on getting reacquainted with Trina. He built a picture of her in his head. Tall, blond, striking.

Trina Odell was everything he wanted in a woman. Independent, with a rich, full life of her own. She liked good restaurants and crowded sidewalks, and so, damn it all, did he.

How would she react to the fact that their first night together after weeks of separation would be spent on a double date with strangers? She was always the life of the party. She'd find Fern Glen...

Well, frankly, she'd probably find it as tedious as he did. He wouldn't give her time to get bored, he decided, he would lavish every spare moment on her. Perhaps she'd like to come into his office. She loved animals, especially dogs.

Trina was a night person. She wouldn't mind being alone during the day if she had him during the night.

He smiled. No problem.

That night a light knock on the door announced a visitor. Lora flung open the door to find her grandmother, two shoe boxes tucked under one arm.

"I'm here to see Victor," she said, marching past Lora.

Lora looked toward the car and the driveway. "Where's Mom?"

"Making a pot roast. She decided Victor will mend faster if he eats red meat."

"But—"

Gram touched her arm. "Hon, don't fret, I know you're taking very good care of Vic. But your mother copes with life's problems by cooking. She always has. She made dozens and dozens of cookies when she was in high school and had a crush on her math teacher. The poor man gained twenty pounds that semester."

"What 'life problem' does Mom have?"

Gram winked. "Man trouble. You know." She nodded her white head in the direction of the den and said, "Is *he* in front of the television again?"

Lora, distracted, said, "What? Oh, Dr. Reed. Yes, go on in."

Man trouble?

Yikes!

Had Dr. Reed said or done something upsetting?

Had her mother?

Far more likely, but Dr. Reed didn't look upset—he'd eaten every bite of the pasta primavera Lora fixed for dinner that night, and Mom couldn't be too angry if she was home cooking up a pot roast, so—

So, what was wrong?

A sudden image flitted across Lora's mind. An image of her mother sitting alone, staring at the framed photo on the wall, a photo of a dead fish.

Dead fish equaled Lora's dad. She was sure of it!

Was her mother feeling guilty over her increasing attraction to this kindly veterinarian? Was she finding that letting go of the past was painful? Was she filled with angst, both for herself and for Dr. Reed, worried she might get hurt or that she might hurt him?

Wow. Like mother, like daughter.

Who would have thought that the woman who refused to allow Lora more than a couple of weeks to get over a failed romance, who had declared that Calvin leaving for Chicago was a blessing in disguise—well, who would have believed that this very same woman would suffer her own qualms about the process of reattaching to someone new?

Okay, what, if anything, should Lora do about it?

Jon appeared just then. He'd taken to washing the dishes, refusing to let her help. She watched as he peeked in the den and then started toward her, his steps sure and bouncy with self-confidence.

She needed to get him to call Trina and hear the "good" news. She needed to stop thinking about him.

He stopped in front of her and said, "What's your grandmother doing in there with Victor?"

"I don't have the slightest idea."

"Looks as though she's got him stringing beads or something."

Lora frowned. Beads?

Jon lowered his voice. "We need to talk," he said. "Let's go out in the back."

"No hanky-panky," Lora grumbled.

"You sound like your grandmother," he said.

"I don't care if I sound like Winston Churchill. No kissing or touching, you know what I mean."

He gazed down into her eyes and said, "I know exactly what you mean. You mean no lying on the grass, no groping, no lips—"

"Exactly. As long as we're clear."

"Absolutely," he said, hands held high. "You're safe with me."

This conversation took place as they walked across the lawn toward the gazebo. Once inside the decrepit structure, Lora sat down and felt suddenly awkward.

He said, "You aren't limping anymore."

"Nope. I heal fast. Super powers. Why were you so upset today when you came into the flower shop?"

"I told you. Heartless people."

"What heartless people?"

"There's no shortage of them," Jon said, sitting right beside her. Why had he done that, why wasn't he sitting opposite her? Should she move or demand he do so? If being close to her didn't bother him, should it bother her?

Why didn't Trina call him? How could she get him to call Trina without tipping her hand?

Jon said, "In this case, the trigger was the lady who owns the wine shop."

"Victoria Pullman? Okay, I agree, she has an attitude problem. Her husband isn't so bad, though. He buys flowers all the time. Victoria does, too, but with her, the flowers are just decoration. Dark red roses when they're having a Cabernet tasting, lemony freesia when it's Pinot Gris. She doesn't really care about the actual flowers."

Jon sat back, long legs crossed at the ankles, arms folded across his chest, a smile toying with his lips. The man had really nice lips. Nibble-able lips. Yummy lips.

Hey, just because she wasn't about to do something as stupid as fall in love with him didn't mean she couldn't appreciate his lips.

He said, "What do you mean? Aren't flowers mainly for show unless you're a honeybee or a butterfly or something?"

She leaned back next to him. Turning her head, she found they were damn near nose to nose, she could feel his warm breath, smell the earthy, manly smell of him and fought a desire to close her eyes and make this moment of near intimacy last.

She said, "I guess so. But sometimes a person will come into the store who really loves flowers. Loves the fragrance, loves the feel of the petals and the dazzling rainbow of colors, someone whose eyes light up just gazing into the refrigerator case and who has the imagination to see each blossom as a fleeting work of art, as proof that life has meaning."

Jon sat forward, his expression going from bemused to earnest. "I know someone like that. He paints watercolors of wildflowers and when he talks about them, he sounds just like you. His name is Nolan."

Lora blinked a couple of times. "Nolan—"

"Nolan Wylie. Lives out near Clam Beach. Do you know him?"

"No."

"Well, he and I were going to hang out this weekend, you know, catch a movie or grab something to eat, but then Trina called—did I mention that?—and informed me she's changed her mind, that a trip up here sounds like a good idea, after all. I don't know what happened to change her mind."

"Are you glad she did?" Lora asked, holding her breath.

"Of course I am."

She exhaled and said, "Good. That's nice."

"Trouble is, I hate to cancel on Nolan. He's kind of shy. But it just now occurred to me, you know, sitting here listening to you go on about flowers, that if you came along, the four of us could go out together."

"Oh, good grief, not you, too," Lora moaned.

"Not me too what?"

"You're trying to match me up with this Nolan character. What? Am I wearing some kind of sign that says, 'Loser'?"

"I don't know what you're talking about. I told you, I had plans with Nolan and since Trina would like to meet you, I mean, I imagine she would like to meet you because you're another woman and Trina loves other women...."

As Jon droned on, Lora tuned out his words and watched his face. The man was a lousy liar. Truly dreadful. His speech pattern changed, he rambled, his hands flew in all directions as he avoided direct eye contact.

She could teach him a thing or two about lying. Keep

it small and believable. Keep the story as close to the truth as possible. Don't use too many words and always, always look sincere and honest.

Heck, any eleven-year-old knew that!

For instance, his statement about Trina loving other women. Did he really believe that?

Maybe he did. Maybe people in love tended to see only what they wanted to see. Look at her and Calvin. For months he'd been getting ready to leave and somehow she'd missed every single not-so-subtle clue. Every weekend he'd bought three or four out-of-state newspapers. She'd beamed with pride: the man was so interested in the world, so well read! Then she'd noticed he scoured the want ads. He'd said he liked to daydream and she'd smiled at this streak of whimsy. He'd talked about the joys of big city life and she'd chalked it up to simple curiosity. He'd talked of making more money and yearning to play the stock market and "be someone" and she'd thought he wanted security for her and their future family. Then he became secretive and purchased new luggage and she'd thought, *He's planning our honeymoon!*

She'd seen what she wanted to see until it was too late. Well, by golly, never, ever again!

Jon was still talking. She caught a word or two about *Trina this* and *Nolan that* and once again diverted her thoughts, thinking she knew exactly how this had all come about. Trina had called and, thinking she knew another woman was interested in *her* man, acted all gushy. Jon realized how much he loved her, but then he remembered the way he'd kissed Lora down to her toenails just a day or so before. Guilt. Then he'd thought of this guy he'd met, this Nolan, and realized a way out of it all.

He was scamming her!

Okay, so what? You scammed him first.

Jon felt guilty. He shouldn't, it wasn't necessary, but he apparently did.

Did everyone she knew assume she was incapable of finding herself a man? Wait, wait! Did everyone she know refuse to believe that she wasn't in the market for one?

She answered her own question with a little nudge of conscience. *Why should Jon believe you've sworn off the male sex when you rolled around in the grass with him? You're sending mixed messages, honey.*

Face it, as far as Jon was concerned, she was a woman on the make and as a consequence, she now had three matchmakers instead of two.

Okay, okay, Nolan Wylie. How bad could he be? She had to assume he wasn't a doddering old man or a wet-behind-the-ears teenager. If Jon liked him he must be intelligent and witty, right?

She could make it perfectly clear to Nolan Wylie that she was not interested in dating. She'd buy her own dinner and shake his hand good-night. She wouldn't lead him on or use him, she had Jon for that purpose!

And, honestly, would she miss the opportunity to see Jon and Trina on a date together?

No way in hell.

She put Jon out of his misery. "Sure," she said. "Sounds like fun. He has to understand this is just a date, right? No chance for romance. I pay my own way."

"Sure."

"Okay."

"Great," he said.

"Is Trina staying here at Dr. Reed's house?"

He looked horrified. "No. Of course not. I discussed this with Victor while you were cooking dinner. I told him I'd hire someone to help him, but he just shook his head. He says he'll be fine, he'll have you. He encouraged me to bring Trina around so he could meet her. Anyway, I'll go back to my apartment. Trina will stay there with me."

Lora felt a surge of emotion she wasn't comfortable naming. She said, "I see."

As they stared at each other, Lora thought how odd Dr. Reed's house would seem after Jon left. She felt a sudden urge to return to her own home, an urge to bury herself in her greenhouse.

Jon said, "We didn't get in even one game of strip poker."

Lora smiled. "Well, it's kind of late to start undressing for each other, isn't it?"

"I'd say·so, yes."

"Dr. Woods, may I see you for a moment?"

Jon looked up from his examination of the wirehaired terrier perched on the table and found Connie at the lab door.

She said, "Please."

"Can it wait a moment?"

"I don't think so," she said, and disappeared, the door closing softly behind her.

"When a woman uses that tone of voice, I know it's time to hustle," the owner said. The man was about fifty and bore an uncanny resemblance to his dog, both of them covered with tight gray curls and possessing dark, intelligent eyes. "Bongo and I will wait right here."

Jon offered apologies, then followed Connie down the hall. Their trip ended in the kennel area.

"She's still bearing down?" he said as he contemplated the little calico nobody wanted. She'd been in labor when he arrived that morning and he'd assumed she'd have her babies the way most of the cats in the world do—in private, taking care of herself and her kittens without human intervention. She'd been in the second stage, where the mother bears down with her contractions. It had been over two hours, and he'd expected to find a litter by now.

"I think a kitten may be stuck," Connie said.

Jon performed a quick examination. Sure enough, a kitten seemed to be jammed in the birth canal, partly out of the vulva. He waited until the calico had another contraction and watched. No progress.

"Get me the lubricant," he said, washing and drying his hands. Connie handed him a pair of latex gloves and the lubricant. When another contraction came, he was ready to firmly grasp as much of the kitten as possible and ease it out, twisting it slightly, coordinating his help with the cat's bearing down.

Within a few moments, the kitten was born. It was a good-sized kitten, too, which explained the problem. The calico seemed overwhelmed by the whole matter and showed no interest in fulfilling her motherly duties. Jon ripped away the membrane around the baby, then taking the clean cloth Connie handed him, gently rubbed the white and orange kitten, clearing mucous from its nostrils, making sure it could breathe before attending to the umbilical cord.

The calico's maternal instincts finally kicked in and she took over. Jon and Connie grinned at each other as the mother's pink tongue lapped the kitten's tiny face and folded ears. The mewing sounded like a mouse squeaking.

"How adorable is that?" Connie gushed.

"I never get tired of seeing this," Jon said, his own throat constricting.

"What about more kittens?"

Jon removed his gloves and very gently palpated the now purring calico. "It doesn't appear there are any more. I think she's just going to have this one jumbo-sized baby. You never know, though, so keep an eye on her, will you? I'd better get back to Bongo. Call me if there's a problem."

He walked back to the examination room wondering how he was going to find a home for the new little family.

Tiptoeing out of Dr. Reed's house before the sun rose, Lora drove to her own bungalow and let herself into the dark kitchen. Mom and Gram were obviously still asleep. Though Lora tended the greenhouse every morning, this was the first time since temporarily moving out that she'd been inside the house, and she looked around with fondness.

And then alarm. No doubt about it, the place was beginning to resemble the home in which she'd grown up. Her mother's flowery apron hung by the refrigerator, her outdoor shoes sat on a piece of newspaper by the back door, all the glass containers that Lora used to store rice and pasta on the drainboard had disappeared and in their place sat a row of ceramic canisters in ascending sizes, shaped liked pears. And what about the toaster? Where the heck was her red toaster?

Wait, were those new curtains? Lora fingered the lacy cloth and suppressed a sigh—her mom had made new curtains in her absence. Lora hated to be territorial, but where were the perky little red-and-white gingham curtains that came with the place? She liked those curtains. And her toaster.

And the chair cushions!

The colors were suddenly subdued. Pastels! Lora's signature red was just a memory. She had to get back home before new furniture began arriving.

Opening the refrigerator, she found a small bottle of orange juice and took a swig. She could see the covered dish which her nose told her held the pot roast Gram had mentioned. She grabbed an apple and closed the door.

Her next stop was the aquarium and the first thing she did was count the fish. All present. Taking the supplies from the laundry room and trying hard to be quiet, she scrubbed algae from the sides, replaced part of the old water with new, treated water and adjusted the pH level.

When she was done, she kneeled in front of the tank and peered through the glass directly into the mysterious world of water and plants all bubbling and swaying nicely thanks to the filter, and wondered what it would be like to swim around in seventy-eight degree water all day, wondered what it would be like to have a three-second memory.

Maybe not so bad. While it was true the good things in life would be too soon forgotten, it was also true the bad things would disappear in less time than it took to blow your nose. There was an appeal to that.

Next, as she did every morning, she unlocked the greenhouse and turned on the lights. The single-paned glass building was old and unheated, cold at this time of day. Rows of beautiful wood benches held dozens and dozens of pots, most of which sported lovely green leaves and little else. Their flowering time was still a good thirty days away.

The row of pots in the middle were the exception. The pots in the middle were flowering, and the blossoms they sported were so exquisite that they literally took Lora's breath away each and every time she saw them.

True red lilies, a shade she'd hybridized after years of failure. The flowers were large and graceful, upfacing, two to four buds a stem, but it was the color that would dazzle the world, a red as deep and true as a red delicious apple.

Lora watered the plants and updated her records. She hadn't heard from her lawyer which seemed odd and made a mental note to call his office. If everything went according to plan, the deal that would introduce this lily to the world market would be signed, sealed and delivered within a few weeks.

This lily was her future. It was her bridge to tomorrow. Not a six-lane bridge, mind you, not even a double decker with a walkway. Just a modest foot bridge that would finance the salvation of the florist shop.

And, it was a secret. The attorney for the purchasers had insisted on this.

She tended the soil, counted the buds and kissed a fleshy

petal before turning off the lights and letting herself back outside. It was still dark, though the faintest pink line near the eastern horizon promised sunrise. She heard a hissing noise and called good morning to Boggle who regarded her from under her neighbor's back porch.

She drove to the store and entered another dark building. It was Friday and besides two funerals and a wedding to prepare for, this was carnation day! Within hours, a dozen elderly men would storm the place, asking for their free carnations, catching sight of Ella Williams and her bright blue eyes. Within hours, Gram could choose the pick of the litter.

Why hadn't anyone ever thought of this before? It seemed such a foolproof way of getting people together! Flowers did that, they celebrated life and death, they assuaged hurt feelings and grief and marked events like birthdays and anniversaries, they coaxed smiles and contentment, they represented the wide world of natural beauty available just outside the modern door.

Who didn't love a flower?

As she worked on the arrangements for the wedding, she had no trouble envisioning the store as it would be someday. More work space, better lighting, a new walk-in fridge and display case. She saw worn wood floors, real trees, antique furniture, orchids and high-end giftware. She could smell the peat moss, envision the old wooden chairs she'd paint and mount on the newly redone walls, each supporting a fall of greenery. She'd been planning this store in her head since she was sixteen; it was far more than a dream.

By eight o'clock, most of the arrangements were loaded in the van for morning deliveries. Lora met her supplier at the back door and took possession of yet more carnations, these a lovely purple and white combination, and for the first time, she wondered how exactly to go about arranging the afternoon…festivities.

By the time Mom and Gram showed up, she had formulated a plan. "Mom, I need you to go to the Lemon Drop Bakery and pick up four dozen cookies," she told her mom before Angela could take off her coat. "I called and they said they'd set them aside."

Her mother looked scandalized. "Why didn't you tell me you needed cookies? I could have baked them last night!"

"Poor planning on my part, sorry," Lora said with a breezy kiss. "Gram, we need napkins and sparkling cider. Three bottles. And little glasses."

"Not champagne?" Gram asked.

"We don't have a liquor license." Besides, it was too expensive and who knew how the seventy- to eighty-year-old male guests would react to a jolt of booze in the middle of the afternoon? "Cider," she repeated.

"What's going on, Lora?" her mother insisted.

"It's a promotion I arranged for this afternoon. I'll need both of you to help me."

Lora's mom looked stricken. "I made other plans. I thought I told you, but maybe I didn't. Oh, dear. If you'd only told me earlier—"

"You would have snuck off with him anyway," Gram said with a wink to Lora.

Snuck off with who? Dr. Reed? Where else would her mother go with a pot roast? Lora felt like buzzing her mother with questions, but she knew too well how pointed inquiries destroyed intimacy. Her mother would talk when the time was right.

Dr. Reed, on the other hand, would no doubt answer any and all questions if just asked, say, over a nice stir-fry!

Lora said, "Gram and I can manage. I'll make deliveries as soon as one of you gets back from the store."

They both left and Lora began shoving tables around, one for cookies, one for cider. Flowers for decoration were certainly no problem, she thought as she drifted snow-white cloths over the round tables.

As she worked, she found herself humming.

Now, where did they keep that old radio?

Chapter Eight

To Lora's delight, her grandmother really got into the whole idea of promoting the flower shop by giving away free carnations. Her mother, back from collecting the cookies, thought the endeavor too expensive and rather foolish. She plunked the bakery box down on the counter and without even taking off her coat said, "It's not like we're made of money, Lora."

Lora narrowed her eyes. "Is that a new coat?"

Angela Gifford looked startled. "This old thing?"

"Mom, that's a new coat."

"Well, maybe."

Lora looked closer. Her mom was wearing makeup. Makeup! And her blue dress didn't look familiar, either. Nor did the happy glow in her eyes.

Lora felt an unexplained stab of...regret. Regret for the husband her mother had lost, the father now faraway, the glow that should have been caused by him but wasn't.

Change sucked.

"Like I said," her mother repeated, hand on the doorknob, "we're not made of money and those cookies and the cider are expensive, to say nothing of the flowers."

"Maybe her secret plan is finally working out," Gram said as she tied on a clean yellow apron.

"You mean with the lilies?"

Lora looked from one to the other of them, her mouth dropping open. "You know? You *both* know?"

Gram tsked. "Did you really believe I thought you were growing drugs in the greenhouse?"

Her mother said, "Honestly, Lora, you've been working with lilies since you were in high school. Now you close yourself up in that greenhouse every morning and half the weekend. It doesn't take a brain surgeon."

"Or a rocket scientist," Gram added. "Plus you got a call the other day from a Mr. Pitt. 'Course you weren't home, being over at Vic's house. Pitt said he was your lawyer."

Lora gasped. "You didn't tell me!"

"I didn't?"

"You didn't tell me, either," Lora's Mom said.

"I told someone." Gram shook her head. "I must have had a senior moment. Sorry, Lora."

"Well, what did he say?"

"Oh, that everything was going well. That there should be papers to sign in a week or two, that the Dutch are anxious. I thought that was some kind of code like the CIA or the Mafia use!"

"It's not a code."

"That's what your Mr. Pitt said. I asked if he wanted you to call him back and he said no I should just tell you and now I have only it's late and I truly am sorry."

Lora balanced her irritation against the relief of knowing there wasn't some kind of snafu and patted her grandmother's arm. "Next time, write it down."

"What's the good of writing something down if you're

not there to see it? So, are you going to tell us what this is all about?''

"It's about one of her lilies," her mother repeated.

Gram turned to her mother. "Why does she need a lawyer for a lily?"

"For a patent," her mother said, looking at Lora. "The Dutch are the biggest lily growers in the world. If they're interested in something Lora hybridized, they would work through lawyers to acquire it, but Lora would have to be the one to patent it because in the United States, only the originator can obtain a patent, not the buyer. Am I right?"

Lora smiled. "I should never try to put anything past you, Mom."

"Damn right," she said.

"The originator has a year to complete the patent. Mine is almost done. Plus, my lawyer talks to their lawyers and I don't have to say much of anything to anyone. Which I like."

"You are amazing."

Lora blinked a couple of times and said, "Thank you."

"Now, if we could only find you a good husband."

"Mom!"

"Okay, okay, just a thought. Are you going to tell me what you came up with?"

"Not yet. I'll show you when the time is right."

"Good enough." She opened the door, took a step outside before turning back. "Your secret is safe with me, honey," she added before closing the door.

"Gram," Lora said, approaching her grandmother. This *is* a secret."

Gram looked wounded. "I know about secrets."

"It's just that I promised to keep quiet—"

Another deep-bosomed tsk was accompanied by a narrowing of the brow and two small hands planted on padded hips. "Lora Rose Gifford. Don't you talk to me as though I'm a child. I do know about secrets. I won't tell anyone

about your flower, I wouldn't even know *what* to tell anyone because you haven't told your mom or me a thing.''

Lora had to admire her grandmother's tactic. Didn't they
always say the best defense was a good offense? ''Okay,
you're right and I'm sorry.'' Seeking to change the subject,
she nodded toward the door. In a conspiratorial tone, she
asked, ''Who's Mom off to see?''

Gram smiled. ''Now, Lora, dear. That's a secret I promised not to tell. You wouldn't want me to go back on my
word, would you?''

''Sure, I would. Yes. Definitely.''

''Sounds to me like a double standard.''

''You think? Come on, Gram, talk.''

''No. Let's get ready for your promotion.''

''But Gram…''

It was no use. Lora capitulated, knowing she could ask
Dr. Reed a few pointed questions that night. Two hours
later, just as she expected the first of the ''carnation men''
to appear, the bell rang. She peered around the counter
expecting to find a gray-haired man waving a Lora Dunes
business card. Instead, she found Jon.

He strode through the store as though he owned the
place, so cocksure of himself that it induced conflicting
feelings of affection and annoyance from Lora. He spared
Gram a smile and a nod, then his gaze caught and held
Lora's. Her heart climbed up her throat and got stuck there.
Producing a small CD player, he said, ''I ran into your
mother at Victor's house. She said you were looking for
something to play music. Victor said you could borrow
this.''

His matter-of-fact delivery seemed to disentangle the
knot in her throat and return things to normal. And hey,
not only music, but a confirmed sighting of her mother
with Dr. Reed! Lora thanked Jon profusely as she took the
CD player and plugged it in. ''What were you doing at
Dr. Reed's house during the middle of the day?''

He handed her a half-dozen CDs. "I was packing up my things. I thought I'd move back to the apartment tonight."

"Oh, that's right, your girlfriend is coming."

"That's right."

"Trina."

His brow wrinkled. "Yes. Trina."

They stared at each other. The short time they'd spent in each other's arms consumed Lora's thoughts. The details came flooding back: the smell of the damp grass, the sounds of the creek, the weight of Jon's body, the urgency and passion of his lips.

His soft voice, his hands…

She suffered an overwhelming and totally irrational dislike of this woman she'd never met, the woman she'd schemed to get to come for a visit.

What a stupid, stupid idea. Fumbling, she selected a CD at random and stuck it in the player.

Jon said, "Nolan is really looking forward to meeting you."

She said, "I can't wait to meet him, too."

"Trina and I will pick you up at seven tomorrow night at Victor's house."

"Your car is too small. We'd better take my van."

"No, I'll arrange something," he said, apparently horrified at the thought of putting the beautiful Trina in a flower delivery van. Well, she couldn't blame him. It wasn't exactly luxurious and lately it made a clanking noise when she turned to the right.

"You know, it's occurred to me that Victor and my mother are getting kind of tight. What's to stop him from telling her that Trina is visiting and that I'm dating some third party, not you?"

"I asked him not to," Jon said.

"Oh. Okay, where are we going?"

"The Brewery," he said.

Lora winced internally. The Brewery had been her and Calvin's favorite hangout. How many bottles of beer and baskets of spicy Buffalo wings had the two of them consumed within its aging walls? She hadn't been there since he left town and she had no plans to return there now. She said, "Pick somewhere else."

"I don't know somewhere else."

"Then I will."

"Okay. Where?"

"I don't know, I'll tell you later."

She hit the play button and they both jumped as the player emitted an earsplitting noise. Jon found the volume button right as Lora did and they both jabbed at it. In the end, the music subdued, they found their fingers entwined. Both of them jerked back and stared at each other again.

Another ring of the bell on the door saved Lora from thinking of something to say.

They both stared toward the front of the store as Arthur Polanski, the man from the dry cleaners—looking rather like a retired schoolteacher in his gray tweed jacket—walked right past Gram and approached Lora. "Hey, chickie," he said with a grin. "I'm here for my flower."

Lora turned her back on Jon's sudden grin. From over her shoulder, Jon whispered, "You and your fixation on older men."

She spared him an over-the-shoulder frown before ushering Mr. Polanski to her grandmother. The two older people sized each other up, Gram with a wrinkled brow, Mr. Polanski from over the top of his trifocals, and Lora traipsed back to the work room to wrap a carnation in tissue paper. Out of the corner of one eye, she watched Gram pour Mr. Polanski a cup of cider.

Within a few minutes, two more men appeared. They both looked vaguely familiar. As Lora wrapped, Gram entertained. Much to Lora's surprise, Jon was still fidgeting with the CD player, this time trying out different albums. She tried to ignore him.

A new bell announced yet more arrivals. Lora couldn't believe the scope of her success. She'd given out about a dozen cards, more or less, and there were about eight people here now. Gram was filling cups, dispersing cookies, her round cheeks flushed, her laughter trilling over the top of the Irish music Jon had settled on. When the bell rang yet again, she glanced up and did a double take.

A small bus had parked in front of the store. A young woman wearing a red smock printed with the words, "Pine Grove Retirement Residence" held open the door. Filing past her were a half dozen elderly men, some with canes and walkers, some on their own, all holding a small pink card Lora recognized as one of the new ones she'd picked up from the printer at the mall and then promptly misplaced.

Not one of the men looked even remotely familiar.

"Quite a rush on your shop," Jon said from behind her.

She had assumed he'd already left. She twirled around and because she was growing a little alarmed by the hordes clamoring for flowers out front and he was grinning, snapped, "What are you still doing here?"

"Watching your booming success." Leaning so close his breath felt warm against her cheek, he added, "Don't you think cornering every old man in the town of Fern Glen for yourself is a little, well, greedy?"

"Go away," she said.

"I want to order flowers for my apartment," he said in an indignant tone with a grin chaser. "Something big and showy for a large table. It looks like you're a little busy, however. Gosh, are you sure these poor guys are up to running around with you?"

"Hush," she hissed. "Go away."

"But my flowers—"

"I'll deliver your flowers later," she said. "Don't you have to get back to work?"

He laughed out loud as he made his way through the crowd, a good head and a half taller than anyone else. Lora watched his retreat, then stared wide-eyed as he held the door for another gaggle of elderly men.

Who were these guys?

Jon's gaze found hers and he winked before exiting.

Gram made her way through the throng. "We need two dozen carnations," she said, brushing flyaway strands of snowy hair from her face. "Lora, I understand the idea of promotion, but why in the world is every single one of these people an old geezer?"

"Well—"

"Where did they all come from?"

Good question, Lora thought. Where *did* they all come from?

Jon swung his duffel bag onto the bed and returned to the living room, pausing to crank up the thermostat as he did so. The furnished apartment was located close to Victor's practice; he'd taken it for that reason, and had lived in it several weeks before temporarily moving into Victor's house. Now he was back and he moved through the spacious rooms with the odd feeling of being totally out of sync.

His condo in Beverly Hills was smaller than this, but held more furniture, especially since he'd taken possession of his father's things and hauled them home after the funeral. Now the place seemed cramped and cluttered and again he was struck by the need to relocate. Maybe he could find an affordable place outside of Beverly Hills proper and commute to work. A place with a yard for a dog, a calico cat and one large orange and white kitten.

He walked into the spare bedroom and made sure the heater vent was open. The northern Californian ocean air was damp and cool and Trina was a hothouse flower. He didn't expect her to sleep much in this room, but he knew her well enough to know she'd travel with several suitcases full of designer clothes and they would require closets and proper humidity of their own. He rolled back a closet door and stared at the lone hanger dangling there and wondered how it came to be left even though he'd been assured professionals cleaned between tenants.

Okay, so he was bored.

Back in the kitchen, he looked in the fridge and found a few cold drinks and a bag of dried-out baby carrots he immediately tossed. It was a far cry from the food at Victor's house. Lora was a great cook, a truly inventive cook, who seemed to add something of herself to every dish she prepared. How did a person get to be that kind of cook? Was it taught or ingrained?

He'd shop tomorrow morning for the essentials, then drive up to the airport and collect Trina, bring her back here. Later, they'd pick up Lora and Nolan and proceed to the restaurant.

He'd taken Nolan a modest pile of clothes to choose from and was admittedly a little curious to see what if any of it Nolan would wear. More important, he wondered what Lora would wear. As many times as he'd seen her, it had always been on an extremely informal basis. She seemed to favor jeans and sweaters, all a little big, all a little old. Except for the dress, the aqua one, the one with the floating skirt and the little straps.

The point was he wasn't familiar with her dating attire.

That's because you've never actually dated her, you moron, he thought to himself as he popped open a cola and stared at a framed print of redwood trees. *You've kissed her, you've talked to her, you've held her, but you've never dated her.*

For a second, he wondered what would have happened if he'd met Lora down in his own neck of the woods, on his own terms. If he'd been unattached. If she'd been less convinced that relationships are doomed to failure. If they'd just been two people walking along a pier and bumped into each other. Would his interest have been piqued by her small stature and flood of dark hair? Would she have taken a second glance at him? Would a chance encounter have given him an opportunity to discover that engaging offbeat streak that ran though her like an unexpected vein of gold runs through a rock?

Who knew?

It was hard to imagine Lora away from Fern Glen. She was as rooted here as her beloved flowers, composed of the very things that made this place beautiful, remote and hard to figure. She would scorn Beverly Hills as much as he scorned Fern Glen.

He moved to the front window and discovered Lora's van parked out on the street in front of the apartment. At the same moment, the doorbell rang and he sprinted across the room to open it.

He was greeted by dozens of yellow flowers, few of which he recognized. He'd never seen so many shades of the same color in the same place at the same time. It was as though a ball of dazzling sunlight floated in the air, and he stood transfixed by the sheer magnificence of it.

From behind the flowers, he heard a small voice. "Help!"

He grabbed the vase as Lora drooped.

He set them in the middle of the round table next to the kitchen. It was startling how much warmth the brilliant bouquet brought to the sterile-looking room.

He turned back to find Lora leaning against the wall. She wore faded jeans and a black shirt, black cross trainers on her feet, the same clothes she'd been wearing earlier at her shop. Compared to the perky flowers she'd hauled up two flights of stairs, she seemed faded. And undeniably pretty in that little-girl-lost way she sometimes had.

"Sit down and I'll get you something cold to drink," he said.

She nodded and threw herself in an armchair.

"Cola, root beer, tomato juice or sparkling water?"

"That," she said succinctly which he took to mean water. As he delivered it, it struck him that this was the first time he'd ever brought her any food—or drink. It was always the other way around. He said, "Do you want something to eat? I have a can of chili. Maybe a frozen pizza—"

"I have to cook dinner for Victor."

"Maybe not. When I was there earlier today, your mother was warming up pot roast. They were deep in conversation when I walked in. I think your plan might be working."

She smiled, which chased away the waif look and brought out the woman in her. "I know. Ain't love grand?"

He pretended to shake his head as though to clean out his ears. "I'm sorry, I must have misheard you. Did you just make a comment about love being grand? You?"

"I know, I'm just giddy that my plan worked. Mom is the kind of woman meant to be in love."

"And you're not?"

"And I'm not."

"How about your grandmother? I figure all the older guys were there as part of some elaborate matchmaking scheme you came up with. Am I right?"

She grimaced. Slumped in the chair, arms and legs flopped this way and that, she looked totally beguiling. Maybe it was the very unpretentiousness of her pose, the unplanned grace she exhibited that she would no doubt deny if it was pointed out to her. He'd noticed it before. The way she sat on a stool or perched on a fence rail, the way she moved through the tall grass, the way she fell to her knees to tuck a blanket around Victor's legs or throw her arms around a dog. All eloquent in their simplicity.

"Where do I begin?" she said.

"Begin with the dozens of old men in your shop."

"I had a plan," she said, sitting up now, anxious, strands of pinned up hair falling in wavy tendrils around her face. "I handed out a dozen business cards to what appeared to be eligible men of a certain age. I told them to bring the card into the shop for a free carnation and to be sure to ask for Ella."

"You figured your grandmother might like one of them?"

"Or two. Or three. Or half a dozen, who knows? Who cares? I don't know if she wants to get married again, I mean, maybe at her age she just wants companionship."

"Maybe, maybe not."

Wagging a finger at him, she added, "It's not as though she hasn't done this very thing to me on a somewhat modified basis for the past few weeks."

"I'm not arguing with you. But when I left the shop there were literally dozens of guys milling about and I saw another retirement home bus pull up as I walked down the sidewalk."

"Well, that's where my plan got away from me." She frowned and he smiled; he couldn't help himself. She said, "I accidentally left a box of business cards at the mall. The man I'd just given one to tried to catch up with me to return the box. When he lost me in the crowd, he decided he'd just bring it in on Friday but when he got back to his retirement home, he told the activity director about it and she decided that she'd help me along by distributing cards to all the other retirement homes. Did you know there were six of them in this area?"

"No, I didn't," he said, smiling broader.

"Well, there are. Five of them decided to make field trips to our shop. We ran out of cookies right after you

left, out of cider right after that and out of carnations before the last busload came in the door. I had to give away
roses. I haven't added it up yet, but this little fiasco cost
us big bucks."

"And did your grandma—"

"No. She thought they were all too decrepit. She's seventy-one years old. Why is she so picky?"

He perched on the rolled arm of an overstuffed couch.
"Why shouldn't she be picky?"

"Because she's seventy-one years old."

He shook his head. "Do you really believe that growing
old means you're not as choosy about who you spend your
free time with? I would think it would be the other way
around. I would think you'd care more."

Lora groaned. "Don't get all philosophical on me. This
is the woman who tried to team me up with a nineteen-
year-old boy a while ago. I've met every young male rel-
ative of every woman in her church. She has no right to
suddenly get discriminating."

He didn't respond. He figured she was just putting the
day in perspective and didn't want to hear him disagree
with her. Instead he said, "The flowers you brought are
beautiful. Trina will love them."

Lora looked toward the table. "I thought she might like
yellow. She seemed like the sun worshiper type. You
know, warm beaches, all that blond hair, honey in her
voice—"

"Her voice? When did you hear her voice?"

Lora stopped talking and stared at him for a beat or two,
then shrugged. "I mean that she probably sounds totally
southern Californian. I've seen enough movies to know the
type."

"That's absurd. You're a prejudiced woman, Lora Gifford."

"I know I am. The first time I saw you, I thought you
were from Hollywood. You looked like central casting had

sent you over to play the role of young heartthrob veterinarian. It was hard to believe you were for real. And your voice! That soft way you spoke to Boggle, was that some secret language you use on suggestible felines?''

It was difficult to know what to do with her when she got like this. The easiest way to shut her up, he knew by experience, was to kiss her. His feet practically tingled with the desire to cover the few feet between them and put this remedy to work. Of course, this reasoning was fatally flawed in that kissing her always led to a host of other complications.

She added, ''You know, now that I come to think of it, you haven't worn your glasses once since that day. What's that all about?''

''Contact lenses. You caught me on a day when I didn't have them with me.''

She rose quickly and came to stand in front of him. They were just about eye to eye, her a little taller as he was sitting down. She peered into his eyes, hers as green as grass, as green as leaves, as green as everything that grew in the earth and reached for the sun. ''Hmm—'' she said. Her thick black lashes begged to be licked.

What an absurd thought! And since when had it ever occurred to him to lick anyone's eyelashes before? It sounded messy...and very tempting.

''I see the contacts,'' she said, her gaze darting from one of his eyes to the other.

He caught her arms. ''Stop, you're making me dizzy.''

''Well all I can say is that you looked damn cute in your glasses, it's a shame you don't wear them more often.''

''Trina doesn't like them,'' he said.

''Oh.''

''And when a person cares for another person, then that person tries to do the things he or she knows pleases the other person.''

She smiled. "Listen to you," she murmured, her fingers brushing his cheek. "How considerate you are."

She was right there. Her lips were so close he could see every detail of them, every little millimeter, even the faint memory of lipstick probably applied hours before but not nearly as attractive as her own natural color. She smelled like sunshine though that was impossible seeing as she'd spent her day inside wrapping flowers. He said, "How much do I owe you for the flowers?" His voice sounded distant.

"You don't owe me anything. Thank you for bringing Victor's CD player. I think I was kind of brusque with you and I'm sorry."

"You weren't brusque, you were overwhelmed," he said, still staring at her lips. When she spoke, her small white teeth peeked through and glimpses of her tongue reminded him of what she tasted like. He felt himself growing aroused. He felt himself itching to pull her into his arms and though he knew it was selfish and unfair when they were both obviously fighting an attraction for the other and when she'd told him point-blank that she didn't want to grow attached to him because he was leaving and she had this hang-up about men anyway, it didn't lessen the desire. It didn't make letting go of her one iota easier.

Oh, yeah, and then there was Trina.

Holding firm, he lifted his gaze to her eyes.

She shook her head as she drifted toward him. His hands slipped from her arms and encircled her torso; he felt her warm breath growing incrementally closer as her face hovered near his. He closed his eyes and waited breathlessly, afraid to make a sound or move a hair, afraid she'd come even closer, more afraid she'd disappear.

He felt her silky cheek rest against his, her breath caress his earlobe. He felt her fingers in his hair, on his neck, on his shoulders. He felt her body pressing closer, her breasts against the insides of his arms and then against his chest, her hips against his knees and then his thighs. One of his hands slid down to her denim-clad derriere and the other strayed up to stroke her face.

"Lora," he whispered. "Lora."

"Shh—" she said, and he could feel her lips move against his cheek.

"I—"

She stilled him again with a fingertip against his lips. He tried to enjoy this intimacy for what it was, but the tension her nearness created threatened to blow off the top of his head. Perhaps this warm encounter satisfied something in her, but all it did for him was cause an agonizing ache.

He put his hands on her shoulders and looked at her again, and this time he saw that she'd closed her eyes and he understood the tacit approval inherent in this gesture because he'd just made it himself. *He could do with her as he wished, for a moment anyway, and she would pretend she was someone else, somewhere else, and let it happen.*

Her acquiescence engendered in him an unholy wave of passion that brought his lips crushing against hers. He caught her body and gathered her against him in a perfect fit, knowing she would have to be dead not to realize the extent of his hunger. And she kissed him back with a vengeance, her mouth hot and demanding as he reached under her clothes and stroked her heated, bare skin. She wasn't wearing a bra, and on their own accord, his hands moved to caress her small breasts. Her nipples felt hard against his thumbs, begging to be tasted if he could ever bring himself to stop kissing her mouth.

Her hands had breached his clothing as well and he felt them glide across his back, over his shoulders, down his chest; the craving to get even closer obliterated all rational thought. Her mind must have raced along the same path.

They hastily fumbled with each other's buttons, hands clumsy but intentions clear, until her breasts pressed against his chest, skin to skin, heat to heat.

How had a kiss escalated to this so quickly? It was as though a firestorm raged through his body and arched into hers. Her skin was hot to the touch and so soft. He plunged his tongue into her mouth and pulled her closer yet. Had any other man felt the delight of her curves beneath his hands and the urgency of her kisses?

Calvin?

Had Calvin touched her like this and then abandoned her? How could a man do something like that to a woman like this?

You will, came a sudden voice in his head that cut through physical sensations like a red-hot spoon through a scoop of ice cream. *You'll leave her, you know you will.*

She'd tried to warn him.

Once acknowledging the problem, he owned it. If this wasn't wrong, why then did she close her eyes, why did she pretend she wasn't with him and why was he talking to himself instead of making love to her?

He pushed her gently away and she looked at him with full, parted lips, half-closed eyes and tousled hair, half-naked and so desirable he knew without a doubt he would never forget a single thing about her and this moment as long as he lived.

"Jon—"

What in the world could he say to her? He finally whispered, "I can't."

She blinked rapidly as though he'd just flicked on a bright light.

"I'm...sorry," he mumbled. "I got...carried away. I forced your hand in this and I'm very, very sorry."

She stared at him, comprehension filling her eyes, her breath catching. In a flurry, she reached for her clothes and held them against her chest with trembling hands, backing away.

He felt like a rotten heel and a fool, a disquieting combination. He knew they were both adults with free will, so why couldn't he shake the notion that he should have protected her from this?

Was it because he suspected all this mattered more to her than to him? Because he had a full, wonderful life in an exciting city with a potential mate and all he really needed to do to make everything all right again was go home and reclaim what he had without leaving Lora's life in tatters? Repeating himself, he whispered, "I'm just so damn sorry."

"Stop saying that," she said softly, looking up at him then, her chin titled at an almost defiant angle. "I'd like to blame you, it would make me feel less of an idiot, but the truth is, I'm the one who started it. You're the one with the steady girl. I should have known better."

"You should have known better!"

She smiled. "Okay, you should have known better, too." She looked down at the clothes bunched against her breasts and added, "Now, look the other way."

He looked the other way as she dressed herself, turning when she said he could. She handed him his shirt which he buttoned as she started speaking again, her voice low and fast and steady.

"This whole thing figures. I'm allergic to cherries," she said, pulling on her shirt hem.

He didn't need to pretend to be confused. "Huh?"

"Cherries. Every time I eat one, I get hives. Nowadays, I don't eat them. It's simple." Staring at him, she added, "I'd wager that if you have to have an allergy, it's not a bad one to have. There are a few chocolate candies I can't eat, an ice-cream flavor or two I've never tasted, and I'm careful what I put on my cheesecake, but besides the fruit itself, that's about it."

As usual, she'd lost him. He waited.

"But when I was younger, I couldn't stand it. Mom told me not to eat cherries so you can just imagine what I craved. It was terrible. I spent every Fourth of July covered with angry red bumps because I couldn't keep myself from trying just one lousy cherry. I always broke out and I always tried again."

"You're comparing me to a cherry," he said.

"Yes."

"I guess I've been called worse."

Her eyes met his. "Jon, cherries are delectable, tasty and bad for me."

He nodded.

She put out her hand. "Friends?" she said.

He took her hand into his. He didn't think it was possible to be friends with her. She was turning out to be rather addictive. Talking with her was always an adventure, kissing her made his heart race, the thought of hurting her was unbearable. Thank heavens Trina was coming tomorrow, thank heavens he would be going home in a couple of weeks. And then the cherry talk got through to him. She'd just told him that she'd craved cherries because she couldn't have them. She hadn't mentioned adoring the way they tasted or coveting their juicy plump flesh. Their sole attraction seemed to be the fact that they were forbidden.

In other words, she coveted being intimate with him because she knew she shouldn't. He was taken, hence he was safe. He was bound to leave this town, again making him safe. The moment he announced he was free—if such a moment were to ever happen—he'd bet a million bucks Lora would vanish like a puff of smoke on a windy day.

And his attraction to her? Was it something equally as glib? Had he wrapped her in a fantasy of his own making?

"Friends," he mumbled.

With a firm nod of her head, she slipped her hand from his and walked to the door, letting herself out without a backward glance.

Chapter Nine

Lora spent Saturday morning making cinnamon rolls for Dr. Reed. Her mother and grandmother had assured her they could handle the store by themselves and she'd taken them up on the offer. It was a rare Saturday off and she'd already been to the greenhouse.

Dr. Reed was hobbling around on his own by now, mending faster than anyone had expected. It was still something of a challenge to keep the bigger dogs from stepping on him and Bow Wow and the cats were constant underfoot threats. Lora locked them all in the backyard when she knew Dr. Reed was up and about as he was now.

Was it possible he could go back to work sooner than expected? Was there anything she could do to facilitate this possibility? She knew his sister drove him back and forth to the doctor's office; maybe she could take over that chore and hear how his progress was going.

As he settled on a stool in front of the counter, she propped his bad foot on a chair. He emitted a huge sigh of relief and it came to her that he was still at least a couple of weeks away from being able to stand in an office and examine animals all day.

Damn. Jon would have to stay.

"More coffee?" she asked.

With his nod, she refilled his cup and sat down on the opposite side of the counter.

She said, "I see from the leftovers in the fridge that Mom brought you a pot roast."

He smiled. "You bet. She's almost as good a cook as her daughter. Those rolls look delicious. And is that heavenly smell sausage? When are we going to eat?"

She glanced at the timer on the oven. "Ten more minutes. So, about Mom. She looked pretty in her new blue dress, don't you think?"

"Very attractive," he said. "She's a lovely woman. Reminds me of you."

"I'm shorter than her—"

"I don't mean in appearance though of course there's quite a resemblance between you two, height notwithstanding. No, I mean that she seems a little guarded when it comes to her emotions, just like you are."

"Me? Guarded?"

"I think so." He peered at her and added, "Take this Trina woman coming up here to see Jon. How does that make you feel?"

Lora shrugged. Dr. Reed couldn't know it, but the mention of Trina and Jon in the same sentence caused her heart to triple beat. How she felt was ashamed—of her part in Trina's sudden visit, of falling into Jon's arms the night before when she'd neglected to do something as rudimentary as wear a bra. Of everything.

She wanted Jon to go home with Trina. She *needed* him to go back to his own life and get out of hers. She said, "I don't feel anything about it."

Running a hand through his silver hair, Dr. Reed said,

"But just a few days ago, I saw him kiss you. Aren't you the teeniest bit jealous of Trina?"

"Why should I be jealous?"

"Because you care about Jon—"

"Dr. Reed!"

"Well, I just thought you might like to talk—"

"Well, you thought wrong," she said, abruptly getting to her feet, upsetting the stool in her haste. She straightened it and added, "Jon and I are…"

"Are what?" he asked gently.

"Friends."

"Does he know that?"

"Of course."

Dr. Reed nodded. "I see. Friends."

"Like you and my mother," she said, hoping to turn the conversation back to something approaching comfortable.

He nodded, his blue eyes thoughtful. Lora knew there was no use trying to pump him for more information—he'd clammed up. The buzzer on the oven went off, and she escaped to the land of cinnamon and yeast, flour and raisins and sugar, to plump sizzling sausages and warm ovens and cold juice and homey smells that almost obliterated agonizing memories of pressing her naked flesh against Jon's. Of his hands, his mouth. His voice…

Almost…

By late that afternoon, she was in a feminine whirlwind, desperately searching through the few clothes she'd brought to Dr. Reed's house for something appropriate for a date. Not the aqua dress. She always felt dowdy in it—well, except for the time she'd worn it to entice Jon and he'd looked at her like she was dessert—

No, not that dress.

Why had she neglected to buy herself something new to wear?

Money. Money went for greenhouse expenses, attorney fees and florist shop bills, not for frivolous things like clothes.

She pictured Trina—tall, leggy, blond, slinky. Lora decided they would go to the Fern Glen Inn for dinner. It might be pricey, but it would impress Trina and she imagined that would please Jon.

What a big-hearted trooper she was! So thoughtful! So kind!

Common sense said she couldn't compete with Trina.

Why did it even occur to her to try?

Because she was so damn attracted to Trina's boyfriend that it hurt. It was like having the flu.

By now he'd picked Trina up from the airport. Were they making love right that moment?

She couldn't bear to think of it.

By now he was in love again and whatever infatuation he'd had with Lora was a memory, probably not one that even brought a smile to his lips seeing as their trysts had been torrid but brief and always frustrating.

Okay, okay, wear what you'd wear on any date—remember Nolan what's-his-name?—and go take a shower.

Pep talk given, she called and left a message on Jon's phone about the location of dinner, then borrowed Dr. Reed's car—the blue van was at the shop being used for Saturday deliveries—and drove to the mall, spending the next two hours tearing through racks of clothes until she found a siren red dress and a pair of outrageous red shoes to go with it, rationalizing to herself that it was only polite to dress up and make Trina feel less conspicuous.

Besides, the dress was short, tight and sexy. At least it was on the hanger.

Back at Dr. Reed's house, she fixed him an early dinner, showered, did her hair, applied makeup and dressed. By six o'clock, she was sitting on the side of her bed, hyperventilating. At six-fifteen, she heard the doorbell and swore under her breath.

How dare Jon come forty-five minutes early, she thought as she stormed down the hallway. How dare he assume she'd be ready and waiting!

Never mind that she was.

"I'll get it," she told Dr. Reed as she passed the den where he sat at a card table someone had set up for him, bad foot propped up on an ottoman, a floor lamp illuminating the surface which was covered with plastic boxes. He was stringing beads on a nylon thread as the gray and white cat watched with a twitching tail. He'd been doing this for days.

She tore open the door. The white cat streaked inside as Gram swept past Lora and started down the hall. "You look great, honey," she added over her shoulder.

Lora closed the door and followed Gram into Dr. Reed's den. "What are you doing here?"

"Your mother and I are baby-sitting Vic tonight while you and Jon go out on a date," Gram said. The dogs had all gotten to their feet and were nudging her hands as the white cat curled around her stocky legs.

Dr. Reed looked at Lora. He winked, which she took to mean that he understood he wasn't to talk about Trina, then he whistled. "Look at you. You're just as pretty as a picture."

All Lora could think of was calling Jon and telling him she'd meet him away from this house where Gram and her mother wouldn't see Trina. The last few days had been kind of nice what with no strange men lurking in the shop, peering at her as though they were contemplating buying a car and deciding if they wanted to give her a test drive.

"Where's Mom?"

"Bad headache. It's just me. Vic, that's a really swift necklace you created. You have talent, my boy."

To Lora's surprise, Dr. Reed put down his pliers and

held up the finished project. It was made with gold and oblong crystal beads, a delicate gold flower suspended in the middle. "Come here, Lora," he said.

As he motioned her to lean close, she held her hair aside and he fastened the necklace around her neck.

"Perfect," Gram beamed.

Dr. Reed said, "You don't have to wear it tonight."

Lora felt tears burn the back of her nose. No way was she going to cry when she'd just finished applying three coats of extrathick mascara, so she willed them away. "I love it," she said, leaning to kiss his forehead, then twirling to find a mirror.

The necklace looked charming, the flower dipping toward what passed for cleavage on Lora's small frame. She touched the flower and looked back at Dr. Reed and the tears threatened again. "Thank you so much—"

The doorbell rang. It was only six-thirty.

Jon and Trina?

Gram said, "Oh, Lora, that's right. Your mother tried to call you this afternoon and warn you, but you weren't home—"

"Just a second," Lora said as someone seemed to lean on the buzzer. She hurried to the front door, her thoughts focused on preempting Trina from meeting her grandmother, but when she tore it open, it wasn't Jon or Trina or even her mother who stood on the porch.

Calvin.

"Great, you're ready," he said as though they'd chatted the day before.

Lora was almost but not totally speechless. She said, "What are you doing here?"

"We'll talk about that over dinner," he said, his hazel eyes traveling up and down her body as though he was a wealthy rancher considering the acquisition of a new filly.

It was no wonder a western image sprang to mind. Calvin might have left Fern Glen wearing a three-piece business suit, but he'd returned decked out like an extra from the set of *Bonanza:* tan cowboy hat so new it seemed to be made of cardboard, spiffy blue shirt with pearl buttons, skintight fancy jeans and spanking new cowboy boots.

"What happened to you?" she asked.

"Montana," he said with a gleam in his eyes that made Lora suspect he might soon burst into song.

"I thought you went to Chicago."

He shrugged a broad shoulder. "At first. It's a rat race there. Montana is where it's at. You'd love it."

"I bet I would."

"You surely would," he said with a wink as he tugged on the brim of his hat. Lora half expected him to throw on a "Ma'am." Instead he said, "You're not acting very pleased to see me."

"I'm still stunned."

"Didn't your mother tell you I was back in town?"

"It must have slipped her mind."

"Well…I am."

"I can see that."

"Your mother told me you were staying here for a few weeks."

"Which explains why you're standing on Dr. Reed's doorstep, but not why you're back in Fern Glen, Calvin."

"Isn't it obvious?"

"No, as a matter of fact, it isn't."

"We'll talk over dinner," he said.

Dinner! *Jon.* She said, "I can't."

"But you must be dying of curiosity about why I'm back."

"Kind of," she admitted. Was it almost seven? Had one minute passed since she opened this door or one hour? She didn't know. She added, "I can't visit right now. We'll talk tomorrow."

He put a hand against the door as though afraid she might try to slam it. Damn intuitive of him. His expression beneath the brim of his stiff hat turned suspicious. "Lora, are you okay?"

"I have to go. It's been…interesting…seeing you."

"Why are you all dolled up?"

"I have a date."

"A date!"

His surprise got the best of her. "Yes, a date," she said smoothly. "Are you so surprised to discover that I'm not sitting on the shelf where you left me?"

"No—"

She took a certain pleasure in saying, "Yes, you are."

"I'll come back tomorrow," he said.

"There's not much point."

"But, Lora, sweetie—"

"Calvin? Stuff it, okay? You left. Now it's time for you to mosey on off into the sunset because I'm just not interested."

"Who *is* he?" Calvin growled.

"*That* is none of your business."

And with that she closed the door. To her great dismay, she found that she was trembling, damn near from head to toe. To her great relief, Calvin left. She watched from inside the house as he pulled away from the curb just as a moderate-sized sedan turned into the driveway.

It looked as though the time she needed to compose herself wasn't going to happen. Right on the heels of seeing Calvin, she would have to deal with seeing Jon and Trina interact, a prospect that didn't seem half as amusing or interesting as it had when she'd coaxed Trina into flying north.

The car door opened and Jon emerged. He must have rented a vehicle for Trina to use while she was here which made sense as his Porsche wasn't big enough to hold two people and a picnic basket let alone four people and at least one major case of nerves.

Lora grabbed her purse and hollered goodbye into the

interior of the house, determined to stop Jon from introducing Trina to Dr. Reed while her grandmother was present.

Jon's welcoming smile kind of slipped off his face when he caught full sight of her. Egad, was the dress that bad? He wore black slacks and a black shirt, a dark gray jacket thrown over both. His clothes looked expensive yet effortless.

What was she doing in a flashy cocktail dress?

This feeling didn't get any better as she caught a glimpse of the off-white sweater and slacks adorning the striking blonde in the front seat.

Jon and Trina were a matched set, perfectly dressed for a Saturday night at Fern Glen Inn's Rib Room, elegant but not ostentatious. Lora realized her dress was over the top but there was no way to go back into the house without arousing Gram's curiosity, so she decided to make the best of it.

Jon caught her hand before she could get into the car. As he leaned close to talk, she realized with a start that she recognized his aftershave. His warm breath, his firm grip, his voice—every detail of him now found a niche in her sensory memory, like tiny keys that fit perfectly into tiny locks, so that his scent was no longer just a scent but a catalyst, evoking other, more intimate moments.

What a disquieting revelation. Here she was coveting another woman's man on the evening of a date with a new guy after telling her old boyfriend to buzz off.

"For reasons that will soon become clear," Jon whispered quickly, "I'm thinking it might be best if we go to a different restaurant. Did you already make a reservation at the Fern Glen Inn?"

Lora admitted that she'd forgotten to call.

"Great. Then let's go to The Brewery. They don't have a dress code. One more eccentric won't attract any attention."

Lora looked down at her beautiful red dress. Okay, maybe the sequins were a little much, but eccentric?

"Not you," he added quickly, as though catching the direction of her thoughts.

"Then—"

"You'll see. Please, get in."

As she slid into the seat, Jon performed perfunctory introductions and Trina threw a "Hiya!" over her shoulder.

Surprise, surprise, they'd already picked up her date, or at least she assumed the lanky man with the long hair and beard wearing a powder blue tux with a pink ruffled shirt was the infamous Nolan Wylie.

"I like your shoes," she said. She'd never actually seen spats in person before.

Nolan had a sweet smile that transformed his face. "Thanks," he said so softly she lip read it as much as heard it. "They were my dad's," he added. "He doesn't wear them anymore."

She returned his smile. The prospect of spending the evening with this gentle man seemed a pleasant thought after spending five minutes with Calvin and reeling over her tumultuous feelings for Jon.

"Tell me about your paintings," she said, and listened avidly as he described his artwork, barely noticing at all the way Trina's hand draped over Jon's shoulder, her beautifully manicured fingers absently playing with the short brown hair touching his collar, laying claim.

The Brewery was loud and raucous on a Saturday night. Jon found a table along the north wall under a picture of five cats dressed in roaring twenties clothing sitting around a table playing mah-jongg. He noticed the way Trina stared at the painting before perching her elegant derriere on a chair and for a second wondered if he should have worried less about embarrassing Nolan and more about impressing Trina.

Nolan, on the other hand, looked right at home in The Brewery. Even his tux blended in with the wide-open dress policy of a restaurant catering to everyone from professionals to college students.

And then there was Lora, adorable in her fanciful red dress, hair adrift on her creamy shoulders, lips painted red and so succulent that it was hard to take his eyes off them. He should be ashamed of the lust he felt for her and was rather surprised that he didn't. He held her chair, catching a whiff of her scent as she sat down.

Then his gaze met Nolan's and he realized he'd overstepped himself, that Nolan had been waiting to seat Lora. Jon instantly felt contrite and smiled to say he was sorry.

As he sat beside Trina, she touched his arm. "Jon, where are the menus?"

"On a chalkboard over the bar," he told her.

"And the wine list?"

"I don't imagine they have one."

"But they do have twenty-six different microbrews," Lora said, which won her an admiring glance from Nolan.

Trina said, "Great. Jon, is this town always so foggy?"

He said, "Uh…no."

Nolan said, "It's foggy on most summer mornings and then the wind comes up and blows the fog away for the rest of the day."

"That's in the summer," Lora added. "In the winter it just fogs and rains. In the fall and spring, like now, it alternately fogs and rains and blows."

Trina said, "How do you stand it? It's wreaking havoc with my hair. I guess for the week I'm up here I'll just do what you do, Lora."

"What does Lora do?" Jon asked.

Lora smiled. "I don't do anything."

"That's what I mean," Trina crooned. "You just let nature have its way, right? I suspect that's all a girl can do up here, just give up."

"Or wear a hat," Lora said. "I have several."

While Jon didn't pretend to understand the way women interacted with one another, even he could feel the tension between these two. Lora's being tense he could understand. She was on the spot, undoubtedly torn between the unresolved feelings between him and her and an uneasiness with meeting two new people. But what was going on with Trina? Why was she being so nasty? Did this have something to do with the way she'd quizzed him on the drive from the airport, wanting to know about the women he'd met up here?

Nolan seemed oblivious to the electricity whizzing past his head.

Jon said, "I think you both have great hair."

"Yours is the color of the wild lupine on the beach," Nolan said out of the blue, turning to face Trina. "Pale, pale yellow. It's very pretty."

"Aren't you the sweetest thing?" Trina said with a trilling laugh. Jon happened to know she'd spent hours practicing that laugh to get the pitch just right. Details like this had always made Trina's lust for fame more understandable to him, hinting at a vein of vulnerability he suspected she tried hard to cover. She waved a hand and said, "Jon, you know what I like, you order for me. See if you can't scare up an Oregon Pinot Noir, you know, like the one we had at Stella's last Christmas party."

With that, she got to her feet and shouldered her purse. For some inexplicable reason, Mrs. Pullman, the beautiful kitty hater, came to mind. He shook the image as Trina added, "I'll be back in a moment or two."

Nolan offered to go after the drinks. After much discussion they all decided on what they wanted and Nolan, repeating the various brew names and the wine name to himself, left.

Staring after Nolan, Lora said, "He's very nice."

"I'm glad you like him."

"He's different. Unassuming."

"I guess."

"And Trina is beautiful."

His collar felt too tight and he rolled his shoulders. "She is that," he said. He wanted to add that Lora looked exquisite, that the red of her dress exactly matched the red of her lipstick, that red was her color and she should wear it all the time.

"So why the change of plans?" she continued. "Why here instead of the Fern Glen Inn? Why did you pick up Nolan before me? What's going on?"

"Nolan called this afternoon and asked to be picked up first. He wanted to go to the door and get you, but he got cold feet at the last moment."

"How cute is that?" Lora said softly.

"Adorable," Jon humphed under his breath. He knew he should be pleased that Lora and Nolan were getting along. He wasn't.

"And we're here at The Brewery because of the way Nolan is dressed," Jon said. "I tried to influence his choices. I didn't have much luck."

"Are you apologizing for him?" she asked, eyes wide.

"I just don't want him to be embarrassed—"

She switched to her know-it-all voice as she said, "How long have you known Nolan, Jon?"

"Not too long."

"I've known him less than an hour and I can tell you right now that Nolan Wylie doesn't care what other people think of him."

"Is that right? Well, Miss Know-It-All, *you* weren't there when he said women didn't like men who dressed like he did."

"What was he wearing when he said that?"

"Jeans with holes and paint spatters. Threadbare flannel."

"And now he's wearing a tuxedo and spats and is very

pleased with the way he looks. I can't believe you don't know that.''

"Well, excuse me. I guess I'm not as tuned in to Nolan Wylie as you are.''

"Apparently not," she said.

"And by the way, you look terrific.''

She opened her mouth and closed it without speaking. Apparently he'd caught her off guard. About time she was the one left speechless!

She finally murmured, "Thanks. So do you.''

Their gazes caught and held. He had the sudden urge to discuss the night before. He wanted to know what it had meant to her. He wanted to examine what it had meant to him.

For instance, had she come on to him for the sole reason that he was unavailable? Was it pride or something more that made him refuse to really believe that? Hadn't he sensed more?

Was he really only one of her damn cherries?

She looked away from him as though uncomfortable. "Are you enjoying Trina's visit?''

"Of course," he said, neglecting to mention the way her constant nitpicking was already beginning to wear on him. The way she'd thought the giant redwood trees were gloomy, the beach desolate, the sunny flowers on his table too gaudy. Should he tell Lora that they'd spent the afternoon apart, him at the clinic and Trina at a hairdresser, or should he leave her guessing?

Who says she cares where you spent the afternoon? his subconscious insisted.

But some part of him thought she might. *Hoped* she might...

Trina returned with Nolan who struggled with a heavy tray. Lora hopped up and helped Nolan settle the tray on the table as Trina perched daintily on her chair.

"This is the only wine they have," Nolan said, placing a frosty glass before Trina.

Jon crossed his fingers that her good manners would kick in and she wouldn't announce with an arrogant wave that she didn't like white wine.

"Thank you," she murmured. Then she leaned close to Jon and added, "How did you ever find this place? You should see the ladies' room, all fussy wallpaper and baskets like a little country shack. And the colors! Mauve and gray, for heaven's sake! That look is so over! After the eclectic decorations out here, who would expect such daintiness in the bathroom? I didn't know decor like that still existed."

"The motto here is not to fix it if it ain't broken," Lora drawled.

"Like the rest of Fern Glen," Trina observed.

Jon tried to think of a way to change the topic.

Nolan sipped his beer and glanced nervously from Trina to Lora. "I like baskets," he finally said.

"Baskets are…nice," Trina said with a condescending edge Jon hoped only he was aware of.

The conversation lagged as a waitress appeared and took their orders. After she'd left and no one seemed able to think of a thing to say, Jon mentioned meeting Nolan at the beach.

Nolan took up the story. Lora smiled throughout. Trina's gaze darted from table to table. Was it his insecurity talking or did each of her glances register another decibel of disapproval?

Why hadn't he just driven them to the Fern Glen Inn? They could all be seated right now at a big round table in front of a fireplace eating prime rib and sipping the proper vintage. Trina would be glowing instead of glowering.

Nolan ended his halting dissertation by meticulously describing his dog, Bill.

"He sounds just like my poor Bitsy," Trina said, zeroing in on the conversation at last. "Bitsy died last week."

"I'm so sorry," Lora said.

"He was old. Still, it was heartbreaking not to have Jon there to help me." Sticking out a lower lip, she added, "Jon, why have you banished yourself from civilization this way?" Without waiting for him to disagree with her terminology, she looked at Nolan and added, "He didn't even know this Victor Reed guy until his dad died and now he thinks he owes him his undying loyalty. Well, what does he owe me? What did he owe poor Bitsy?"

"Bitsy died in his sleep," Jon said calmly, his gaze straying to Lora's face to try and figure out what she thought of this conversation, but she was staring across the room. "Ellen and Bob both called to reassure me that they helped you deal with the details," he added, turning slightly to follow the direction of Lora's gaze. She seemed to be looking at a man wearing a huge cowboy hat. "There wasn't really anything I could have done for him."

Trina shook her head. It was her way of telling him he'd missed her point.

Well, he knew how emotional she was about her late dog and he truly was sorry that he'd missed being there to comfort her, but her open denouncement of him in front of his friends made him want to tote her back to the airport.

Trina's lovely face fell into another petulant pout. Had she always been this temperamental? She put her bronzed hand on Nolan's arm and said, "I'd love to meet your little pooch while I'm here."

Nolan looked bewildered by her request but finally muttered, "Yeah. I mean, sure."

Music started to play and Trina underwent another transformation, something he'd found charming in the past. "Dance with me, hon," she said, caressing his cheek. This time, her mood swing annoyed him until he glanced at Lora and found her whispering in Nolan's ear.

He felt a surge of adrenaline that had nowhere to go. Lora was free to cozy up to any man she wanted, but…with Nolan? Within an hour of meeting him? Was she that man crazy? First she'd flirted with the cowboy across the room, now it appeared she was nibbling on Nolan's ear.

Jon popped to his feet and grabbed Trina's hand. "You're right, let's dance," he barked, leading her onto the dance floor which was really just a space in the middle of the room cleared of tables and chairs. She filled his arms for the first time since their welcome hug at the airport. As she rested her cheek against his shoulder, his gaze met Lora's and they both looked away.

Chapter Ten

There was something in Jon's glance that made Lora distinctly uncomfortable and she lowered her gaze at once. The evening so far had been one disquieting moment after another. Trina was a testy, snotty jerk, Nolan was sweet but dull and Jon was acting downright weird.

And now Calvin. What in the world was he doing here?

It's his favorite haunt, why wouldn't he be here?

Egad! He isn't going to come over this way, is he?

Lora turned back to Nolan. "Kiss me," she said.

She'd already hurriedly explained that she needed him to pretend they were lovers because of an old boyfriend. He'd looked baffled then and he looked even more baffled now.

"Hurry," she said briskly, and without giving him another moment to dither, planted her lips on his.

It was like kissing a flour tortilla.

Calvin cleared his throat over their table. "Lora?"

She looked up.

"This is your new...friend?"

Lora introduced the two men who eyed each other suspiciously. She glanced at the dance floor, found Jon scowling at her, and once again lowered her eyes.

"I can see that you've moved on," Calvin said.

"You didn't leave me much choice," she mumbled.

"So, I guess there's no point in my staying around."

"Wait a second," she said, alert again. "Are you saying you came back to Fern Glen because you thought you and I could pick up where we left off?"

"I came to take you to Montana with me," he grumbled. "I came to marry you."

The noisy restaurant faded away.

As she gazed up at Calvin, she felt the oddest sense of peace fill her body. Calvin had deserted her, he'd hurt her. She'd been stumbling around in the dark, but now it was as though the heavens had opened up and sent a shaft of pure light to illuminate her heart. Calvin wanted her back. Residual pain seeped away as she looked her former fiancé in the eye. "I don't believe you," she said.

He smiled in an *aw, shucks ma'am* way. "I knew you'd be surprised."

"That's hardly the word for it."

"So?"

"Calvin, if I didn't want to move to Chicago, what makes you think I suddenly want to move to Montana? The same problems that existed between us then still exist, only more so because now I don't have any feelings for you."

"This fancy dude has filled your head with—"

"Oh, give it up, will you? I barely know Nolan but I'd still rather marry him than you. Why don't you saddle up and go back to Montana? Round yourself up a nice cowgirl but be sure to warn her that you'll only graze in her pasture as long as the mood hits you."

She turned purposefully away. After a few minutes in which music and voices came back into focus, Nolan whispered, "The cowboy left. Are you okay?"

Tossing him a reassuring smile, she said, "I'm fine. Never better. Listen, I'm sorry about the kiss, but thanks for helping me out. You know, I've been thinking. I'm going to renovate my flower shop pretty soon. I'd love to cover the walls with original watercolors. Jon told me how talented you are. I could act as a middle man and sell your paintings in my store. What do you think?"

"Cool," Nolan said, and they clicked beer steins like old friends.

Lora gazed around the boisterous restaurant, full of bonhomie for the whole world—even Calvin—until her eyes met Jon's. So long peace and tranquillity, hello fidgety unease.

As they stared at each other, another shaft of light pierced her consciousness and she actually looked heavenward to see if she could find a hole in the ceiling.

No hole, no light, just biting realization.

She loved this man.

Heaven help her, it was true! She loved Jon Woods.

Telling Calvin to take a hike had been a no-brainer because of that. She wasn't the fierce, independent woman she'd just congratulated herself on becoming.

She was just a silly woman in love with the wrong man. Again.

The poets have falling in love all wrong.

Lora decided this as she arranged carefully prepared Sterling Silver roses in a box for some lucky woman's fiftieth wedding anniversary.

Love wasn't about roses, however, or birds chirping or violins playing or chocolate. Love was about misery.

She'd been in love four times in her almost twenty-five years. Once beginning when she was eleven, a woefully unrequited event that lasted most of junior high before the object of her affection moved out of state with his family; again in high school 'til her boyfriend started dating her

best friend behind her back; once with Calvin for unspe-
cified reasons that currently mystified her; and Jon.

All dismal failures.

She could see the others for what they represented: infatuation, security, escape, stupidity. But the feelings she
harbored for Jon were different.

So different. Night and day different. The other guys
had all been less than she'd built them up to be in that
blasted imagination of hers. Jon was more. He was funny
and kind and smart and loving...every time she talked to
him, every glance they exchanged, every moment they
shared just made it all...more.

How could he love Trina? Of all the wonderful women
in the world, how could someone like him find someone
like her worth talking to, let alone loving? And if he didn't
love her, then why was he squandering his emotions on
her?

She thought she knew the answer. Trina was the kind
of woman a man like Jon wanted to rescue. He thought
her vanity masked insecurity. He thought if he dug deep
enough, a real human being would emerge like a phoenix
from the ashes of hair spray and cashmere.

The phone rang, interrupting these miserable thoughts,
and she found herself talking to her lawyer, Horatio Pitt,
who actually sounded jovial. They made an appointment
for the coming Monday.

At last, things were happening! She needed to keep focused.

What if Jon came to his senses and dumped Trina? What
if he came striding into the store right this second and
vowed his unrelenting love? Oh, my, what if...

What if?

Jon was a big city boy with plans to buy into a partnership, plans to expand his horizons. He hated Fern Glen
and even if he talked himself into tolerating it because he
was madly in love with her—sigh—sooner or later he'd

get bored and restless and leave just like her father had left her mother, like Calvin had left her.

How had she lost sight of her original objective? Not Jon, not love, not marriage. The shop.

She, too, had plans. Plans to expand, plans to renew. Her future was right here within these four walls and even if she talked herself into moving away to embrace another person's dreams, sooner or later she'd grow restless and become unfulfilled. To save Jon, to save herself, she needed to squelch these dangerous romantic notions right now.

Still, each and every time the door opened, she looked up to see if it was Jon. Every jingle of the phone made her heart lunge. She wanted to see him so badly it hurt.

It didn't help that her mother was so preoccupied that she hung up on a customer or that Grandma cast Lora sideways glances and made that deep tsking noise. Something was up with the two of them, but Lora was too caught up in her own drama to ferret it out.

It didn't help that Dr. Reed called and told her that he had ordered a catered dinner for the coming Saturday night, that he was feeling better and he wanted to celebrate, even hinting that he had special news to share. Would Jon and Trina be there, too? Of course they would.

By late afternoon, she'd had as much of her own fears as she could stomach and decided to take Nolan up on his offer to drop by to see his watercolors. First she made the last of the deliveries, then she drove to the beach and along the winding road he'd told her about the night before.

Nolan's house was in a small cul-de-sac, surrounded by tall grasses, stunted trees and pots of flowers. Lora parked behind a new car and walked around an old truck toward the house. A woman's laughter stopped her in her tracks, and she shrank back against the truck. She *knew* that laugh!

Trina! Of course, the car was her rental. What was she doing here?

Meeting Nolan's dog. Calm down...

Lora looked longingly at her own car. Was it possible to sneak away without being seen? No way did she want to see Trina. While she stood trapped in indecision, Nolan and Trina came around the far corner of the house, arm in arm, a dog frolicking about their feet. As Lora watched, they stopped walking and kissed.

And kissed. And kissed.

Lora held her breath as her heart sank down to her feet. Why had she connived to get this hoochie up here? What was Jon going to think when he found out that his vacuous starlet had set her sights on Nolan?

The dog barked and Lora thought she'd been discovered, but no one looked her way, not even the dog. This mutt was never going to win the watchdog of the year award. He barked again and Trina knelt down and picked him up. He rewarded her with a face wash. Trina giggled and called him "Bitsy."

Lora suddenly understood that it wasn't Nolan Wylie Trina wanted.

It was his dog.

Jon strode right past Lora's flower shop, denying the urge he felt to open the door and peek inside just for a glimpse of her.

His step faltered as a vision of her in that spectacular red dress came to mind. Her sparkling eyes, glossy hair, tantalizing bosom. The memory of the slight weight of her breasts in his hands, their softness, his desire, her mouth.

Then he recalled her whispering to Nolan and talking to the cowboy and he realized when he left Fern Glen, she would eventually fall in love and marry. Men liked her— how could they not? She was mending, he could see that, letting down her defenses...but she was not for him.

Didn't mean he had to like it.

With a deep sigh, he stepped into the wine shop, relieved to find no sign of Mrs. Pullman. A middle-aged man with graying blond hair stood behind the counter ringing up a customer's purchases. Eventually, he walked over and introduced himself as Frederick Pullman.

"I'm Jon Reed, your cat's veterinarian," Jon said, waiting for a reaction.

Fred Pullman shook his head. "Kiki's dead. Run over by a car. Victoria said it happened right after I left town. I've been sick about it ever since I got home."

Dead? Okay, an unexpected twist! Should he play along? Jon tried to think of what he would want Fred to do if their roles were reversed. He said, "The cat isn't dead. In fact, she wasn't run over. Your wife brought her in for a checkup and when I told her she was pregnant—"

"Pregnant? Really! Well, that explains Kiki's big tummy, but why would Victoria say she was dead?"

Diplomatically, Jon said, "Your wife doesn't like cats."

"I know," Fred Pullman said sadly.

"I mean she *really* doesn't like cats. You have two."

"Two? You mean Kiki had a baby? Just one? I can hardly wait to see it! Does Victoria know?"

Jon looked around the now empty store. "Let's sit down for a moment and talk," he said.

The week dragged by. Being at Dr. Reed's house without Jon was miserable, especially since Dr. Reed brought his name up on a frequent basis. Furthermore, Lora didn't know if she should call and tell Jon about Trina two-timing him with Nolan or let him find out on his own.

Meanwhile, Dr. Reed steadily recovered. He started talking about going back to work for the first time since she'd come to his house. She heard him discussing various patients on the phone with Jon and she knew that after the dinner party on Saturday night, he would no longer need her care.

She'd assumed it was Jon who had come to visit one night, and she'd run down the hall, stopped to gather her wits, and then casually entered the den, just to find Dr. Reed and her mother in deep conversation. She'd turned away, happy and sad at the same time. That night she'd tried to call her father, but he was still out of town.

She missed Jon. She missed talking to him, feeding him, watching him. The days seemed colorless, like diamonds leached of their dazzle, one following the other with a plodding certainty that left her numb. The very fact that he stayed away told her he was finished with Fern Glen, with her, and she was almost glad for his practicality.

Things were ending as she'd always known they would so why did it hurt so much? Why didn't anything ever work out? Where were the happy endings?

And then she remembered Dr. Reed and her mother.

Lora got so involved watching the caterers set up for the party on Saturday evening that she barely had time to dress before the doorbell started ringing. Wearing the aqua dress, she ushered in Dr. Reed's friends, employees and family.

Her mother and grandmother arrived together, Gram in a bright yellow dress and Mom looking sleek in black. Her mom seemed wired and Lora began to wonder if this party might have another agenda, say, an engagement announcement. Gram barreled into the den and helped herself to a glass of bubbly while Lora opened the door again and found herself facing Jon.

Their eyes locked as they both stood frozen. Finally, Jon stepped into the house. He leaned down and kissed her cheek in greeting and she made her arms stay by her side where they belonged instead of springing around his neck as they ached to do. What would he do if she blurted out that she loved him? Run? Shake his head? Look at her with pity? She looked behind him to greet the dreaded Trina.

"She's not here," he said, guessing the train of her thoughts. "She won't be coming."

Lora nodded, trying her best to look surprised.

Again they stared at each other and again she fought the intense yearning to hold him, to kiss him, to tell him she'd made a mistake, she'd fallen in love, he had to stay, he had to love her back. If only he would give her some sign…

But he didn't. He moved off down the hall as another couple arrived. Lora barely registered their presence let alone their identities.

The party progressed in a lively manner with Dr. Reed making his way through the crowd with the aid of a cane. The buffet-style dinner was delicious and yet Lora noticed her mother barely ate a bite.

When she caught up with her grandmother, Lora whispered, "What's wrong with Mom?"

"She's nervous. This is a big night for her. For all of us," Gram said, nibbling on a Teriyaki meatball.

"Why? What's going on?"

"Nothing, dear." Lora's gaze happened to lock on Jon in that instant, and she watched him for a second, unobserved, feasting her eyes on the gorgeous hunk of male flesh that had unknowingly kidnapped her heart and would be taking it to Beverly Hills when he left. Hopefully, it would eventually find its way back to her. Maybe someday she'd need it again. She knew from experience, for instance, that it made a dandy pin cushion.

Losing Calvin had been a blow to the pride as well as the heart. Losing Jon without ever having had him felt like losing her skin.

Dr. Reed waited until everyone was finished eating before raising his voice. "I have an announcement to make," he said, looking straight at Lora's mother, who clutched Gram's hand with white knuckles.

"I'm feeling damn good," he said and everyone laughed. "My foot is practically mended, but even better, thanks to the little gal who came to help me in my time of need, I got to know a remarkable woman. Lora, thank you for introducing me to your...grandmother."

Huh?

Lora gaped at Gram, who patted her hand and whispered, "Didn't you guess?"

"No...I...but he's...younger..."

"Honey lamb, he's only ten years younger than I am. You were trying to match me up with geezers twenty years my senior! Get with it, this is the twenty-first century!"

"But what about Mom—"

"Oh, Vic's been a doll with your Mom, listening to her, advising her. He's such a dear, wise man."

Victor's voice rang out again as he added, "Elloise, let's share the good news. We're getting hitched just as soon as we can."

As the assembled guests all issued a spontaneous sigh, Gram made her way to Dr. Reed who put his arm around her plump shoulders and squeezed her. She looked up at him with a grin on her face and he kissed her forehead.

They were a perfect match; Lora could see that. Still, she swayed on her feet.

Jon appeared at her side.

"That's a twist," he said.

"Definitely." She looked at her mother, afraid she'd find her face reflecting major disappointment, but her mom just stood there looking toward the hallway as though at any moment she expected the doorbell to ring.

The doorbell rang.

Lora almost jumped out of her shoes. Her mom looked her straight in the eyes and said, "Lora, it's truly amazing, but sometimes things do work out perfectly, sometimes it

pays to follow your heart,'' and hurried away. Casting Jon
a bewildered look, Lora hurried after her.

By the time she caught up, her mom had opened the
door and was in the action of embracing a tall man with
gray eyes and a full head of graying black hair.

"Dad?"

Lora's mom turned to face her. "We've been seeing
each other, Lora. He's been staying in a motel. We didn't
want to say anything to you until we were sure we wanted
to try again. Now we're certain. Isn't it wonderful?"

Her father smiled at her and opened his arms.

Her first thought was this: *No way. You can't just waltz
back into our lives...well, maybe you can hers, but I'm
not that easy—*

And then she found her face buried against his shirt and
his strong arms grasping her, she heard him say her name,
she felt her mother's hand smooth the back of her head,
she felt a hurricane of emotion tear through her innards
like a Cuisinart tears through a carrot, reducing it to mulch
in less time than it takes to make a wish.

Jon heard Lora whisper, "Dad." Between that and the
look of rapture on Angela Gifford's face, it wasn't too hard
to figure out the identity of the man with the smoky eyes.

He watched the family drama play itself out from a dis-
tance, feeling like a voyeur, but unable to look away. In
the other room, he heard Victor and Elloise discussing
plans to marry immediately. He hadn't seen that one coming, but guess what, he hadn't seen a lot of things coming
lately.

Apparently he was about as perceptive as a gutted fish.

With one last look in the den where Lora and her parents
had retreated for quiet conversation, he let himself out of
Victor's house. It was time to go.

A voice halted him and he turned to find Victor, walking
well now, the cane more or less for stability.

"Congratulations on your engagement," Jon said.

"You aren't leaving already, are you?" Victor called.

"As a matter of fact, I am."

"Not for good?"

"No, I'll stay through the week and help you get back up to speed at the clinic."

Victor nodded absently, then said, "Where's Trina?"

"Trina moved on," Jon said tersely. He didn't want to talk about Trina.

"Good," Victor said. "Now you can pursue Lora Gifford without any distractions."

Jon wrinkled his brow.

"Hell, boy, why in blazes do you think I got both of you to live in my house? I sized you two up the minute I saw you together, way back at the hospital. You were made for each other."

"Is everyone in this town a matchmaker?" Jon grumbled.

"There's love between you two," Victor insisted.

Love? Jon couldn't afford to even entertain such a thought. Sure, he lusted after Lora, but love her?

"Don't waste it," Victor warned.

"You forget I'm not the only one involved," Jon said. "There's Lora to consider, as well. We both have full lives and unfortunately, they don't exist in the same cities or even in the same state of mind. Sometimes, I'm not even sure we're from the same planet."

"Poppycock," Victor said, turning away.

Lora buried herself in her greenhouse. The rest of the world was too crazy to handle but in here, lilies bloomed and faded in predictable progression. Hybridizing took place according to strict procedure. Miracles occurred occasionally as with the creation of the red lily, but just as often the steps forward were minimal and took years to

translate into tangible results. There was something en-
during and reassuring about it all.

Not like the tempest that raged inside her at the very
thought of Jon even though she tried hard not to think of
him at all. It wasn't until the greenhouse door squeaked
open and Jon appeared framed in sunlight that she realized
she'd been waiting for him.

"May I come in?" he asked.

She nodded. This was it.

She'd already moved out of Dr. Reed's house and back
into her own, her mother had departed with her father, her
grandmother was assembling a trousseau and planning an
elaborate honeymoon. This was the final act in a bizarre
production of matchmaking gone askew and love that
wasn't meant to be.

Trina with Nolan. Mom with Dad. Gram with Dr. Reed.
Calvin on the prowl for a cowgirl. Jon with a clean slate.
Her with her dreams.

She was kind of anxious to get it over with so she could
go join a nunnery.

Jon shut the door behind him. As he approached, she
had the sudden urge to chase him out of the greenhouse.
Until that moment, this place had been a sanctuary, somewhere he'd never stepped foot in. Now he'd ruined it.

Admiring one of her lilies, he said, "Your grandmother
told me you created these beauties. They're stunning."

She murmured, "Thank you."

"You hybridized them, right? Pollen from one flower
spread on the stamen of a different flower? Germination
through the style to the ovary? Ultimately, seeds to harvest,
new plants with characteristics of each parent plant, bulbs.
It can take years to affect each change."

"You know your plant biology," she said.

"Amazing what the Fern Glen library has to offer."

Now, why did he look all that up? So he could break
her heart a little more thoroughly when he left? She said,

"It takes the new lily two or three years to bloom, so it takes that long to know if you have something or not."

"I don't think I have that kind of patience," he said.

"I have tons of patience with plants. It's people I get impatient with."

A warm smile lit his eyes. "Your grandmother said the true worth of this lily is its color."

Why were they talking about the lily? Well, why not? It was better than talking about their relationship. "Growers have been looking for an upfacing true red oriental for years," she said. "Plus while most lilies bloom in about one hundred days, this one takes about sixty-five and doesn't need a heated greenhouse. Makes it easier and faster to grow. If I could reduce the pollen so it didn't mess up a wedding gown, it would be worth even more. That's what I'll work on next."

"Your grandmother said you patented this lily and are soon going to sign a contract with the Dutch mafia."

Lora smiled at what she had to assume was her grandmother's idea of a little joke. She said, "I'll receive a hefty chunk of change plus royalties."

"That's what she said."

"Gram's idea of keeping a secret is lowering her voice when she talks," Lora said without anger.

"She knows I care about you. But why don't you just sell the lily yourself?"

Lora patted the soil around a still-to-bloom pink lily as she said, "The Dutch will propagate this lily in tissue culture labs. They'll clone millions of them and grow the bulbs in Chile. In about four or five years, this lily will be everywhere. I couldn't do that on my own."

Jon moved a step closer and added, "I hear your mother skipped town and left you in total charge of the shop."

"She and Dad are starting over again," Lora said, staring at her feet, at the wooden benches, at the bins of potting soil...anywhere but at him. "All I have to do is protect their investment while they do it. The store represents their past and my future.''

''You have a lot at stake here,'' he said softly.

She took a chance and met his gaze. ''Everything,'' she said. ''I can't leave. I won't leave.''

''Won't leave,'' he muttered and she came so close to admitting she loved him that she had to actually bite her tongue to keep the words from spilling out.

For what good would those words do? If he loved her, wouldn't he say it? Wouldn't she sense it? How could she admit to feelings that deep when it seemed likely he didn't share them? She just couldn't.

''Your future in Fern Glen is as important to you as my future in Beverly Hills is to me,'' he said at last, his breath warm against her cheek, but his words like icicles. They implied his final acceptance of the fact that both of them were wedded to their own goals. He was right, but the words froze her heart and the next statement came close to shattering it even though she knew it was coming.

''I came to say goodbye,'' he said.

Tears sprang to her eyes. She mumbled, ''I know.''

He wiped away a tear and said, ''Don't cry, sweetheart.''

She shook her head as the tears tumbled willy-nilly down her cheeks. Closing her eyes, she felt Jon gather her close, but she wasn't falling for that old trick and she resisted melting against him, resisted allowing herself to find refuge in his strong arms. His arms without his heart, without a future, were no refuge at all.

''Did you know that Victor's plan all along was to throw us together?'' he whispered, his breath ruffling her hair. ''That's how we both ended up living at his house.''

Figured. She said, ''It didn't do us much good, did it?''

He held her tighter. ''If he hadn't, we might never have gotten to know one another.'' She felt his warm, soft lips graze her forehead. A tilt of her head and she knew he'd claim her mouth....

And they'd soon end up on the dirt floor, heedless of the consequences, enraptured and lost in each other.

It sounded so tempting to just let it happen....

No. No, no, no. It would do neither one of them a lick of good. She stepped away from him and said, "I'm sorry."

Jon handed her a handkerchief. After a moment, he added, "Trina is with Nolan. She went there after our crazy double date. I...I didn't feel amorous...well, not toward her, anyway, so she stormed off—"

Holding up one hand, Lora said, "Don't tell me this."

His eyes looked bewildered as he said, "I thought you'd want to know."

"Why? Trina doesn't have anything to do with you and me. I don't think she ever did."

"Listen, Lora. I could call you or come visit—"

"Don't make me into another Trina," she said.

"And what does that mean?"

"It means I don't want to be the next woman you hide behind. This is it. It was fun—"

"Oh, I get it. You're talking about cherries again."

He was irritating the blazes out of her. Hadn't he seen her fall apart when he said goodbye, hadn't he seen the pain in her eyes? Didn't he realize that one of them had to remain realistic? She said, "You're just a big, juicy piece of forbidden fruit. Nothing more."

He looked stunned by her comments and she wished she could take them back, but at this point, everything seemed more or less academic. He was leaving, she wasn't. Same old, same old. All she really wanted was for it to be over, for him to go away.

He said, "Was that cowboy another damn cherry?"

Cowboy? "You mean Calvin?"

"*That* was the infamous Calvin?"

''In my defense, the cowboy look is new. Anyway, he's no cherry. More like a cherry pit.'' Desperate to end the torment, she added, ''Well, thanks for coming by. Good luck and all that.''

Before she knew it, he was gone.

Chapter Eleven

Jon intended to drive straight through town on his way south, but at the last moment, detoured to the beach. He'd already said goodbye to everyone at the Animal Clinic and he'd stopped at the wine shop to see how Kiki and her kitten were doing. Turned out they now had a cozy little box under the cash register. Mrs. Pullman, on the other hand, had departed for parts unknown.

Personally, he thought Fred Pullman had made the right choice. Cats were a lot more faithful and loving than some women. Take Trina. *Please…*

As jokes went it was an old one, but as woman went, an absent Trina was a good Trina. How a woman could have changed so much in a few weeks still boggled him. He almost felt sorry for Nolan.

He thought about all this as he trudged across the dunes toward the hard-packed sand. Once he reached it, he took off at a run. He'd spent the past two weeks coping with the tatters of his personal life by jogging on this beach every day and it had gradually gone from therapeutic to invigorating. Today, after the trauma of saying goodbye to

Lora, he knew he needed some kind of release before sitting in a car and mindlessly driving…home.

Home.

Lora. The most maddening woman he'd ever met. A world class pain in the neck.

After a mile or so, he found a dry log washed up high on the sand, and he sprawled next to it. He knew he should get back to the car, but the warm sun on his face and the cool wind whipping his hair felt good. Birds wheeling overhead brought a smile; even the empty beach held a new fascination.

All these random thoughts were nothing but diversions so eventually his mind made the loop and came back to Lora.

Lora and her blasted cherries. Lora and her accusation that he'd hidden behind Trina. Lora and her tears.

Lora. Always Lora. From the first time he'd set eyes on her and entered into one of their crazy conversations it had always been Lora.

Good lord, what was he going to do without her?

Those tears. What had they meant? What would she have done if he'd kissed them away? The truth, he admitted, was that he hadn't trusted himself to kiss away her tears because he knew the next time he kissed Lora would be the last time he ever kissed any woman without thinking of the one he couldn't have. The only way to escape wanting her was to leave Fern Glen for good.

At least he hoped that would work. Trina's arrival sure hadn't catapulted him back into his own life; in fact, it seemed to have done the exact opposite. It was just that she'd changed since he'd left, turned superficial, whiny….

Not like Lora. Not funny with a sarcastic streak. Not determined but good-hearted. Not so desirable she took his breath away nor so annoying he wanted to kiss her to shut her up.

Kiss her to make her listen, kiss her to…

Kiss her because he couldn't imagine not kissing her. Kiss her to show her how he felt, to acknowledge that he knew how she felt, how the two of them had to kiss each other or face sudden death, there was no choice, there hadn't been from the very start.

The truth stole over him the way the fog sneaked up on the beach: quietly but with bold persistence.

The truth was Lora.

Trina hadn't changed. She was exactly the same as she'd always been.

Jon stood so abruptly he tripped over himself in the soft sand, hitting his shin on the log as he toppled to the beach. Standing, he hopped around on one foot until he fell again, and this time an elbow got whacked. As he lay in the sand, leg throbbing, rubbing his elbow, swearing under his breath, staring up at the pale blue sky, everything suddenly seemed extraordinarily clear.

Lora. It all began and ended with…Lora.

He felt an odd sensation growing in his gut, pushing toward his throat until a laugh erupted from his mouth. His whole body shook.

Finally, he crawled to his feet and got himself under control, but the control couldn't last, wouldn't last because he knew that up until this point his life had been a quiet river. Now, it seemed, a dam had just burst upstream.

Running back to his car, startling flocks of seagulls along the way, he shouted as loud as he could.

"Trina hasn't changed, you nincompoop! You have! You're the one who changed!"

Well, duh…

If there was one thing Lora knew how to do it was muddle through. With her mother and father out of town and Gram making plans for an extended honeymoon cruise, she had to hire help for the shop. Gloria, the woman she settled on, was good with customers and anxious to learn about flowers, but as yet had ten left thumbs which meant Lora was in charge of all floral arrangements.

The hours were long but that was okay. What else did she have to do with her time? Think? No thanks.

What was the point? Thanks to Dr. Reed she knew Jon had returned to Beverly Hills to arrange financing to buy into the partnership. She hoped that eventually Dr. Reed would stop updating her on Jon's progress. She wasn't sure she could stand the thought of hearing about his next love affair. No. Definitely not.

But as she worked on an arrangement of pink marguerites in a pink ceramic bootie, she had to admit there was a niggling thought that kept running through her mind, inspired by the words her mother had uttered: *Sometimes you have to follow your heart.*

Was it really so important that she redo this particular flower shop? If her folks lost their investment in this place, was it her fault? She hadn't created the financial woes of the store, was it mandatory she bail them all out?

There was no clear-cut answer. She knew neither of her parents would want her to sacrifice her happiness for their store, but somewhere along the line the store had become hers, as well, and she'd worked so hard to keep it. In its current dilapidated condition, she wouldn't be able to give it away, her parents would suffer a huge loss and even if Lora wasn't to blame, she'd feel responsible.

But it was more than just money.

What if she sold the shop and moved to Beverly Hills? Would Jon even want her? They hadn't parted amiably; she'd been surly and short-tempered, he'd been obtuse, she'd said nasty things and he'd walked away.

Just as important, what would she do once she was there? No way the lily money would go far in that high-rent neighborhood. She'd have to work in someone else's shop and delay her dreams of making something special out of almost nothing. And greenhouses. Where would she find a greenhouse to work in? Did Beverly Hills even have greenhouses?

Would loving Jon compensate for what she'd be giving up?

Of course it would, but he'd never mentioned love, not once. He'd never asked her to join him. He'd danced around the edges of coming back to visit, but there'd been nothing concrete....

Yeah, well, who didn't give him a chance to say anything concrete? she asked herself. Who accused him of trying to hide behind her like he'd hidden behind Trina and how in the world did she know he'd hidden behind Trina and not just finally toppled onto what an idiot the woman was?

Lora stuck the marguerites in among the sprigs of fern with a vengeance. *She was the one hiding.* Hiding behind Calvin's deception, hiding behind her father's desertion, afraid to try again because it hurt so much to fail and when you were in love with someone the way she was in love with Jon and didn't know how he felt. It was absolutely terrifying. Of course she was hiding. It was safe in the shadows.

But it was lonely, too....

The bell over the door rang and for a second she waited to hear Gloria's voice call out a greeting and then she remembered Gloria hadn't come in yet. Dropping the flowers in a heap, she ducked around the corner in time to find a uniformed man wheeling three large boxes on a dolly. "Where do you want these?" he asked.

She wasn't expecting any deliveries and these couldn't be floral related anyway because she took those at the back door. "Over here," she told him and watched as he unloaded the boxes which didn't have a return address or their contents stamped in plain sight. Once he'd left, she found a razor knife and sitting on the floor, opened the first box.

Cherries. Baskets of them. Huge, plump, so red they were almost black. She took a deep, deep breath. *Jon...*

No doubt who sent the fragrant cargo. The doubt lay in knowing how it had been intended. Or was there any doubt? Had she hurt Jon to the point where he'd stooped to sending tiny missiles of retaliation? The thought brought tears.

Expecting more cherries, she slit open the next two boxes. One contained dozens of packages of cortisone anti-itch creams and the other a bevy of antihistamines.

She stared at them, confused at first, comprehension slowly dawning as the bell over the door rang again.

She looked up with a sense of the inevitable. Sure enough, Jon Woods walked through the front door, his tan newly revived, his hair once again sun-streaked. A couple of weeks in southern California and he'd gone back to looking like a movie star. Offering her a hand, he pulled her to her feet.

For a second they stared at each other. For a second, Lora thought of playing it cool, of waiting to find out what he had to say, where he stood. What if she spoke first and he looked horrified? What if she inched out on that perilous branch and it broke under her weight? For a second, she took a mental step back and then her emotions, fired to a fever pitch by his mere presence, pushed her into his arms.

And he caught her.

"I can't believe you're here," she murmured as she wrapped her arms around his neck, kissing his warm skin, drinking in the smell and feel of him as though this might be her last chance to do so. Caution? *No. No, no, no.* The time for caution had come and gone.

"I couldn't stay away," he said stroking her hair before cupping her face and kissing her cheeks, mouth, eyelids with the same wild abandon she felt. When his lips finally claimed her mouth, Lora knew she would go wherever Jon wanted, do whatever he wanted, she was his, her heart was his and holding back now seemed not only foolish but impossible.

At last, he held her at arm's length as if to study her. He was wearing his glasses and she smiled as she gently took them off in order to see his eyes more clearly. At last, she said, "I guess Trina was right about the glasses."

Laughing, he picked her up, twirling her around until lowering her back into the haven of his arms. Their lips met again. His mouth was as eager as her own, and even though there were so many words that needed to be said, it was enough for the moment just to kiss and be kissed.

"To hell with the flower shop," she mumbled at last.

His eyebrows shot up his forehead as he stared at her. "That's a fine way to talk after all the work you've put in here. No wait," he added as she tried to explain. "I have something to tell you."

Heart in her mouth, she waited.

"I love you," he said, his voice catching as though he'd never said the words before, as though he could barely believe he was saying them now. "I was lying on the beach, staring at the sky and it came to me like a gift of some kind. I love you. That's why I sent you the cherries and the itch cream and the antihistamines. If I'm bad for you, baby, then I suggest you apply plenty of topical creams and ointments and get used to the itch, because I'm not going away unless you force me to. I love you. And I think you love me."

"Oh, Jon—"

"I'm not done," he said, putting a finger across her lips. "You know," he added with a mock frown, "I've had this trouble with you before. You're a tad argumentative, did you know that?"

She shook her head and kissed his finger. "I wasn't going to argue," she said.

"Good. Because the only effective way to shut you up

is to kiss you and I hate to think of a whole lifetime spent kissing you.''

''Do you really?''

''No. I guess I don't.'' To prove it, he kissed her again. Sometime later, she said, ''You were going to add something.''

''Oh, yeah. I just bought into the veterinarian practice. I'm a partner.''

''I'll move to Beverly Hills,'' she said quickly. ''I love you, too. I've loved you for ages. I can't bear to be apart from **you**. I'm sorry I hurt your feelings, I'm sorry I called you a cherry, I was trying to—''

''Protect yourself, I know, I know, but that's all over now, it's too late for protection, Lora, we're in this for better or worse no matter what happens. And I sincerely hope you don't move to Beverly Hills because I'm moving up here. It's Victor's practice I bought into. Someone has to take care of his animals while he and your grandmother sail the seven seas!''

''You don't have to—''

''See, that's the odd thing, Lora. I know I don't have to. I *want* to. Not only for you, but for me as well.''

''But what about your career? What about your life? You'll have to start over up here. I can't ask that of you.''

''My life is right here and I don't remember you asking me for a thing.''

''But—''

''There you go again,'' he said, shaking his head. ''You just can't help yourself.''

''Very funny, but—''

He quieted her with another kiss. ''Don't you get it, Lora?'' he whispered against her ear. ''This is the point where our lives merge. This town is part of us. Part of you and me. I'm a land owner here. I plan to build a home with a greenhouse in the back. I plan to build a tree house by the creek. This is where I want to get married, this is where I want to raise my children.''

''You want to get married?'' Lora gasped.

He smiled into her eyes. ''That's right. As a matter of fact, I'm currently taking applications for the position of partner-for-life,'' he added in that soft, secret voice Lora had first heard weeks before, whispered to a cat to calm it down, to work magic on frazzled nerves, to induce calm and hint at untold secrets.

The voice that carried a promise on the wings of a caress.

''Let me show you my qualifications,'' she said, drawing his head down until their lips met.

And she did.

*   *   *   *   *

If you enjoyed what you just read,
then we've got an offer you can't resist!

Take 2 bestselling
love stories FREE!

Plus get a FREE surprise gift!

Clip this page and mail it to Silhouette Reader Service

IN U.S.A.	**IN CANADA**
3010 Walden Ave.	P.O. Box 609
P.O. Box 1867	Fort Erie, Ontario
Buffalo, N.Y. 14240-1867	L2A 5X3

YES! Please send me 2 free Silhouette Romance® novels and my free surprise gift. After receiving them, if I don't wish to receive anymore, I can return the shipping statement marked cancel. If I don't cancel, I will receive 6 brand-new novels every month, before they're available in stores! In the U.S.A., bill me at the bargain price of $21.34 per shipment plus 25¢ shipping and handling per book and applicable sales tax, if any*. In Canada, bill me at the bargain price of $24.68 plus 25¢ shipping and handling per book and applicable taxes**. That's the complete price and a savings of at least 10% off the cover prices—what a great deal! I understand that accepting the 2 free books and gift places me under no obligation ever to buy any books. I can always return a shipment and cancel at any time. Even if I never buy another book from Silhouette, the 2 free books and gift are mine to keep forever.

209 SDN DU9H
309 SDN DU9J

Name	(PLEASE PRINT)	
Address	Apt.#	
City	State/Prov.	Zip/Postal Code

* Terms and prices subject to change without notice. Sales tax applicable in N.Y.
** Canadian residents will be charged applicable provincial taxes and GST.
  All orders subject to approval. Offer limited to one per household and not valid to
  current Silhouette Romance® subscribers.
  ® are registered trademarks of Harlequin Books S.A., used under license.

SILHOUETTE *Romance*

COMING NEXT MONTH

#1726 HER SECOND-CHANCE MAN—Cara Colter

High school outsider Jessica Moran could never forget golden boy Brian Kemp's teasing smile—or the unlikely friendship they'd shared when she'd helped him heal a sick dog. So when Brian walked back into her life fourteen years later, with another sick puppy and a rebellious teenager in tow, Jessica knew she was being given a second chance at love....

#1727 CINDERELLA'S SWEET-TALKING MARINE— Cathie Linz

Men of Honor

Captain Ben Kozlowski was a marine with a mission! Sworn to protect the sister of a fallen soldier, he marched into Ellie Jensen's life and started issuing orders. But this sassy single mother had some rules of her own, and before long, Ben found himself wanting to promise to love and honor more than to serve and protect.

#1728 CALLIE'S COWBOY—Madeline Baker

When Native American rancher Cade Kills Thunder came to her rescue on a remote Montana highway, Callie Walker was in heaven. The man was even more handsome than the male models that graced the covers of her romance novels! Would Callie be able to capture this rugged rancher's attention...and his heart?

#1729 THE BOSS'S BABY SURPRISE—Lilian Darcy

Soulmates

Cecilia Rankin kept having the weirdest dreams, like visions of her sexy boss, Nick Delaney, soothing a crying child. But when her dream began to come true and Nick ended up guardian of his sister's baby, Celie knew that Nick really *was* the man of her dreams.

SRCNM0604